SUGAR HEART

SUGAR DADDIES #7

CHARITY PARKERSON

--Warning: This book is intended for readers over the age of 18.

Copyright © 2018 Charity Parkerson
Editor: Vicky Reese
ISBN: 978-1-946099-43-3

 Created with Vellum

INTRODUCTION

On the surface, Cortland and Driver are perfect for each other. In truth, they're a one-night stand gone wrong just waiting to happen.

When Cortland first met Driver, Driver was homeless and messed up in the head. None of that mattered to Cortland. He's drawn to Driver's strength. For someone who's always felt helpless and weak, Driver's scary possessiveness is like a warm blanket. That doesn't mean Cortland has any intentions of getting tied down.

Driver has wanted Cortland from day one. The problem is Cortland is older, richer, and out of Driver's league in every way. When Cortland offers Driver a no-strings-attached one-night stand, Driver jumps at the chance to use the night to—finally—win the elusive man. He never expects the night to reveal he never knew Cortland at all.

After Cortland disappears the next morning, Driver will have to fight like he never has if he hopes to woo the man back. It'll take every skill he possesses. But a love like theirs is worth risking everything.

ONE

The lights were on inside Driver's place. Cortland shoved his hands in his pockets and stared at the door, reciting every pep talk known to man. So much had happened in the last twenty-four hours. He'd met Keegan, Detroit's super sexy friend from New Orleans. Cortland had watched as Keegan charmed Driver into smiling and dancing. Jealousy ate at Cortland's gut and it didn't matter he knew it was stupid. Keegan was obviously still in love with his ex, Omen. The biggest wow of the day was Driver had kissed Cortland. Cortland brushed his fingertips across his lips. He could still feel Driver there.

It had been nearly a year since the first time they met. At the time, Driver had been homeless, and

Cortland had simply been following orders, delivering meals for Micah. Driver's homeless state meant nothing to Cortland. Cortland had been there himself many years ago. Driver had been unwelcoming and cold when Cortland had shown up with a meal from the mission. Cortland hadn't let that get to him. He tried to never let anything get to him. If he let one emotion in, they all tried bursting through the wall he'd built around his heart and mind years ago. Unfortunately, while Cortland had been trying to wear Driver down, taming him like a wild dog, it was Cortland who'd lost himself.

Now, Driver worked for Micah, had his own place, and no need for Cortland at all. Yet, Cortland continued finding ways to insert himself in Driver's life. They'd pulled off a huge feat today. Micah's first major fundraising event had been more successful than Cortland could've dreamed. He should be elated. Instead, Cortland couldn't get past that one detail of the day. Driver's kiss wouldn't leave his mind. It lingered on Cortland's lips. Ate at Cortland's mind. In a cookie-cutter subdivision, where every red-brick home looked the same, and in the middle of the night, Cortland stood there frozen with lust and fear.

"Cort?"

Cortland spun at the sound of his name. Driver headed his way with his dog, Sam, pulling him forward. A young guy who couldn't be more than twenty-one walked at Driver's side with a miniature Schnauzer on a leash. Cortland glanced between the house and Driver. He didn't know how to explain standing outside the man's home this late at night. No doubt he looked like a crazy stalker. He was, but that was a moot point.

"Hey." He gave Driver a small wave while still trying to think of an excuse for being there.

The young dark-haired guy glanced Driver's way. "I'll talk to you tomorrow, Driver." He gave Sam at a pat on the head. "You too, Sam." He headed across the street without looking Cortland's way.

"See you, Jonah," Driver said, sounding absent and not watching the kid go.

Cortland closed the distance between them and went down on one knee to love on Sam. The huge dog was a mix between a golden retriever and a German shepherd. He was a biter but also fiercely loyal. Once Sam had accepted Cortland, the dog had become Cortland's favorite animal. He shamelessly used the dog now as a stall tactic.

"Hey, sweetie. How's my favorite baby?"

"Don't let Bear hear you say that. He'll keep ruining your shoes."

Driver wasn't saying anything Cortland didn't know already. Micah and Wyld's tiny dog had a jealous streak a mile wide. Anytime Cortland came home smelling like Sam, Bear shit in his shoes. He was up to four pairs completely ruined now.

"It's past midnight."

Cortland didn't need the reminder he still had to explain his presence. His nerves were a complete mess. "I know. There's something I wanted to ask you."

"Me or Sam?" That was a fair question since Cortland never looked away from Sam.

"You."

"Okay." Driver sounded understandably confused.

Cortland took a breath and stood. He met Driver's stare. "If I asked you for one night with no strings—like come tomorrow it didn't happen, and we're still friends afterward, would you accept?"

Driver didn't show an ounce of emotion. His features never twitched. "Yes."

Cortland gave him a short nod. "Okay."

Driver's gaze never wavered. "Are you asking?"

"Yes."

"Then we should go inside," Driver said, heading for the door.

Cortland followed. He loved walking behind Driver. It wasn't uncommon for him to find reasons to drag his feet and enjoy the view. As someone who'd been recently homeless, it was possible Driver might not seem like a huge catch to some. Cortland saw what counted. Driver was solid and brave. Cortland was neither of those things. In fact, if anyone could see inside his mind, they'd steer clear of him. Not that it mattered. People still avoided him. He didn't go out of his way to be friendly. Cortland didn't want anyone to get close, except Driver. Even still, he wanted the man's friendship and his body, but he couldn't engage the man's heart. If so, Cortland would destroy him. No one needed that sort of ugliness in their life, especially someone amazing like Driver.

Driver unlocked the door. Cortland followed him inside. The house was bare of most comforts. When Wyld had rescued Cortland from the streets years ago, he'd gone from having nothing to everything in one night. Driver wasn't the same. He was still struggling to regain everything he'd lost. The man had a roof over his head again, but not much else. There was an old recliner in the living room and

5

a stack of books in the corner. He didn't own a TV yet. In the kitchen, Cortland watched as Driver removed Sam's leash and filled his water bowl. Not a word passed between them. Cortland eyed the cabinets. Driver had two of everything. Two plates, two glasses, and two bowls. Cortland was willing to bet, if he opened the drawer, there'd only be two forks, spoons, and knives.

With Sam taken care of, Driver met his gaze. "I haven't been home long enough to take a shower yet. You should join me."

The fear gripping Cortland's throat made it impossible for him to use his voice. He nodded instead. Even though he was scared shitless, Cortland had shown up with determination in his heart. He cared too much about Driver to be weak. This one time he wouldn't fail. No matter the cost.

Driver took his hand. Cortland's lungs filled with air as their palms met. No one ever touched him. He fought the urge to pull away. Driver's thumb stroked his hand, as if he felt Cortland's panic, and he sought to comfort him. This was an insane plan. Cortland didn't know what he was doing here. He couldn't back down. They'd only shared that one kiss. How had he landed in this position?

Inside the bathroom, Driver fired the shower to

life. It was a small space. They'd be right on top of one another. Cortland couldn't breathe. The moment he thought he might make a run for it, Driver turned. Their gazes met. Driver's hungry blue stare always set him at ease. There was peace in possessiveness—like taking the reins from Cortland's hands. Driver took a step closer. Cortland locked his knees, so he wouldn't bolt.

"I have you," Driver said, as if he could hear Cortland's racing thoughts. The distance between them got smaller. Driver's gaze never wavered. His hands found the hem of Cortland's shirt. The material moved upward. Driver's fingers skimmed his bare skin. It didn't hurt. In fact, Cortland's mind went silent. This was why he was here. He couldn't go the rest of his life not knowing what Driver's skin felt like against his. Fantasies weren't enough any longer. He'd go back to them after tonight. Even if nothing else stood between them, Driver was too young for him. The man had too much to offer someone else. He deserved someone whole. But just once, Cortland had to know. Tomorrow, he'd return to his sketch book and solitude. Tonight, Driver was his. For once, Cortland would be brave.

CORTLAND'S SKIN WAS FLAWLESS. That was the only thought Driver would let penetrate his brain while he stripped each of them bare. As he dragged Cortland beneath the water with him, he held tight to his surprise. Cortland was there. He'd made an offer Driver never expected. One night was a start. It was more than Driver ever believed would happen. If Driver had any sense, he would have said no, and forced Cortland to confess any feelings he had for Driver. The thing was, Driver was in love with Cortland. He had been for a long time. Cortland had done more for him than anyone alive. More importantly, he'd shown up. Every single day, Cort had been there through homelessness and his redemption. Cort hadn't treated him differently no matter how little he'd owned or crazy he acted. Without fail, Cortland always looked at him exactly as he did now—like he'd never met anyone he wanted more. Damn, it was intoxicating.

Driver watched his hands as he soaped Cortland's body. Cortland stood still, barely seeming to breathe. Driver kept his touch light. Cortland looked fragile. Delicate. Driver's hands looked tan and rough against his skin. He washed every inch of Cortland. When he was done, Cortland's chest heaved as if he'd run a mile and his cock kept straining to get closer. Driver shampooed his own hair while doing his damnedest not to rush. The instant he closed his eyes and ducked beneath the water, Cortland struck. His hands landed on Driver's hips with the lightest touch. The space between them disappeared. Cortland's lips found his in the sweetest kiss. Driver's breath caught in his throat. This man, he was Driver's heart. Their erections bumped as their tongues met. At the contact, he felt Cortland suck in a hiss against his tongue. A moan rose in Driver's throat at the sensation. He reached between them and palmed their cocks as he walked Cortland backward against the wall. A gasp escaped Cortland as his back collided with the cold shower wall.

Driver pulled away. "No. We have all night. I'm not rushing." He quickly rinsed the shampoo from his hair and switched off the water. No matter how hard he tried not to look Cortland's way, hoping to cool down, his gaze kept colliding with the man's sexy amber eyes. Cortland was always quiet and serious. Solid. His presence gave Driver peace while at the same time drove him crazy with desire. He held Cortland's stare as he toweled off the man's body, drying his skin. Cortland never smiled or looked away. Driver felt Cortland's intensity to his soul.

As Driver led Cortland into his bedroom, and shut Sam out of the room, he fought the urge to apologize for only having a mattress on the floor to offer. He'd been buying things as he could afford them, but it was slow going. Micah had offered to furnish Driver's house, but Driver still had his pride. Now, he kind of wished he'd at least let the man buy him a real bed. He had literally nothing to offer someone like Cortland. A man who lived in a multi-million-dollar home and had a savings account that made Driver choke just thinking about it.

If Cortland cared about his furniture or anything other than Driver, he didn't show it. His gaze never wavered from Driver. "You should be with someone like that boy from outside," Cortland said, surprising Driver with his line of thought. While Driver had been worried over Cortland's opinion of his bedroom, Cortland had been worrying about something completely different.

"I don't want anyone else," Driver admitted as he sat on the mattress and towed Cortland forward. He kissed Cortland's thigh. His gaze flipped upward. Cortland stared down at him with flushed cheeks and serious eyes. "No one looks at me the way you do. I'd be cheating myself by chasing anyone else. You should come down here."

With his hands braced on Driver's shoulders, Cortland straddled Driver's lap. The moment their skin met, the breath stuttered from Driver's lungs. No one could understand what it meant to him for Cortland to be there, touching him. The man already owned his heart. He knew Cortland wanted this to be one night and then return to being friends. The thing was, they'd never been just friends. Driver hadn't truly accepted that before today. He'd been paired up with a guy named Keegan at Micah's charity event. In the brashest way possible, Keegan had point blank asked Driver if Cortland was just a friend or if he was only saying that. Before that moment, no one had ever called him on his bullshit. It wasn't that he meant to lie to anyone other than himself. He just didn't want to ruin the relationship they had. After Keegan's question, Driver realized he was losing his shot by not trying. He'd kissed Cortland the first moment he had him alone. Driver thought he'd ruined things with that kiss. It seemed he hadn't. Maybe this one-night agreement was a desperate move on his part but fuck it. He wanted Cortland. Driver would do anything.

"I'm insanely terrified right now."

Cortland's softly spoken confession melted Driver's heart. Many times, in Driver's life, he'd been forced to make cold and calculated decisions. Cortland made him feel different. Protective. Human. "I've got you. You don't have to even think. Just feel." As Driver made the claim, he rolled, tucking Cortland beneath him. His mouth found Cortland's. Cortland's short nails bit into his shoulders. Driver wanted to move slow. He craved dragging things out and being as methodical as possible. The problem was it was Cortland, and Driver had wanted him for too long. The moment their tongues met and stroked, Driver lost the will to show patience. His hips automatically rolled, seeking more of Cortland. The sensation of his dick massaging Cortland's nearly snapped his mind. Everything was so much more than he'd fantasized. Each brush of skin punched him in the chest. His emotions were so intense they threatened his sanity. The way Cortland moaned and writhed beneath him made Driver wonder if Cortland felt the same.

"Please?" Cortland begged against his lips, causing his heart to skip a beat. He'd never make Cortland beg. He should be the one pleading with Cortland.

Driver tore his mouth away and dug for the

condoms and lube he had stashed beneath a pile of clothes next to his bed. As he suited up and coated the condom in lube, Driver's mouth got away from him. Suddenly, it mattered more than anything that Cortland understood he didn't have condoms sitting around for just any random guy who agreed to fuck him.

"I've been trying to work up the nerve to get you right where you are for a while. That's the only reason I was prepared."

Even though Cortland couldn't look more aroused, his usual seriousness didn't waver. "You don't have to explain. I came here to throw myself on your mercy and I wasn't the least bit prepared. Just desperate to have you."

An unexpected smile snapped to Driver's lips as he lowered himself onto Cortland. "I don't understand why two people so obviously made for each other have such a hard time finding a place in our heads where we're together."

Cortland's intense amber gaze moved over Driver's features. "Because you should be with someone who can offer you more than I ever could. I'm just being selfish tonight."

"That's enough of that," Driver said, covering Cortland's mouth with his. As far as Driver was concerned, Cortland's claim only further proved his point. If asked why he'd never begged Cortland for a chance, he would've answered the same way. No one, especially someone as amazing as Cortland, deserved to be chained to someone half insane like Driver. But like Cortland, Driver was selfish. He would take this night. Tomorrow would bring whatever it brought. Driver would face it then.

Driver nipped at Cortland's lips and kissed him deeply. He wanted the sting of their kisses to linger on Cortland's lips when he left here. He palmed Cortland's cock. Driver needed Cortland as on edge as he felt. Cortland flattened his hands on the wall behind his head, and lifted his hips, seeking more. His open struggle to get closer fueled Driver's lust. Cortland didn't hide how much he wanted this. It was the sexiest sight Driver had ever witnessed. Driver craved more. He wanted forever.

Without warning, Driver shoved Cortland's knee higher and pushed his way inside the man's ass. He froze as Cortland's greedy body sucked him deeper. The way Cortland tensed and gasped scared the hell out of Driver. He didn't want to hurt Cortland. His eagerness had him rushing more than he should.

"I'm sorry. I'll slow down," Driver rambled, trying to make it better.

Cortland met his gaze, looking half crazed. He spoke through clenched teeth. "Shut the hell up, Driver, and fuck me." Cortland's words were like a sledgehammer to his thin wall of self-control.

Driver's mouth slammed down on Cortland's with enough force he tasted blood. Cortland pulled at his hair, demanding more. Driver bit his way down Cortland's neck and chest as he snaked his arm beneath Cortland's knee and impaled the man with his dick. Over and over again, Driver drove home, pumping inside Cortland. He was so tight it was almost painful—like Cortland hadn't been with anyone in years. With his forehead pressed to the center of Cortland's chest, Driver stared down between their bodies, watching as Cortland stroked himself. Every detail of the moment was overwhelming. His balls drew up tight. Cortland gasped for air. He was too close to blowing apart. Driver didn't want this moment to end. Panic stole his breath. He didn't want Cortland to leave. Not yet. He needed to come. It was too soon. His heart needed Cortland more than his body needed release.

He pulled out. A sound came from deep in Cortland's chest—like Driver had ripped out the man's soul by pulling away. He wasted no time sliding down Cortland's body and swallowing

Cortland's cock. Cortland pushed deeper, taking his pleasure. Driver didn't slow. He licked and sucked, allowing Cortland to fuck his throat. His scalp stung as Cortland held tight to his hair and strained against him. The sexiest moan Driver had ever heard caressed his ears as cum flooded his mouth. When he felt Cortland's dick have its last twitch, he surged forward, taking the man's ass once more. This time, there was no slowing or mercy. Driver heard or saw nothing. His every sense was focused on finding release. If he'd ever experienced anything like being with Cortland, Driver couldn't recall it. Pleasure crawled up his shaft. Driver kissed Cortland like he'd die if they stopped. The pressure beating against his crown exploded into wave after wave of ecstasy. His chest felt tight and heavy as he pumped the condom full of cum. Driver worried he'd explode. If Cortland didn't feel how much Driver loved him in that moment, Driver didn't understand how he missed it. He'd never cared so much about one person before in his life. Countless times a day, Driver scared the hell out of himself with his own intensity. Yet he'd never been more terrified of himself than he was in that moment. With their bodies connected and his heart a mess, Driver feared his reaction if Cortland immediately rolled from his bed and left. Maybe the loss would be the push that finally sent him over the edge. Or, just maybe, losing Cortland's affection would be the thing that finally killed him. No doubt, he'd find out soon enough.

CORTLAND COULDN'T STOP KISSING Driver. He knew he should get dressed and leave. After all, he'd only asked for one night. They had to be for just one night. Driver didn't understand exactly how fucked up Cortland was in the head. This man was a good man. If he knew, he'd stay with Cortland and that was the unfairest shit Cortland had ever heard. Cortland couldn't do that to Driver. But still, he didn't stop kissing him. His body hummed with pleasure. The sensations on his skin had nothing on his heart. His soul wept for Driver. He was so fucking in love with Driver that it ate at him every second of the day. He wanted to tear at his skin like the worst of addicts at the thought of never touching Driver again. In that moment, he couldn't pretend Driver wasn't under his skin. Maybe later he could return to that lie. Right now, Cortland wondered how he'd live without him.

Driver rolled to the side, bringing Cortland with

him, and snuggling close. Cortland's heart screamed in denial that it was over. This was real love though. That meant sacrifice. Loving Driver meant letting him go, so he wasn't forced to realize Cortland wasn't functioning at a normal human level. When Driver disappeared inside the bathroom, Cortland knew he should make a run for it. His body wouldn't budge. Driver reappeared with a warm wash cloth. Cortland could only watch as Driver cared for him. It seemed like he should be embarrassed or say something. He definitely needed to say goodbye. None of that happened. Cortland's gaze never wavered from Driver's beautiful blue stare. It was like his brain chose to soak up every detail of the moment, intent on torturing him with the memory for the rest of his life. Whatever the reason, Cortland didn't leave. When Driver settled in beside him and tugged Cortland into his arms, Cortland let it happen.

For what felt like hours, Driver took turns between holding his stare and stealing kisses until his eyes finally slipped closed. Even then, Cortland didn't look away. He watched the way Driver's lashes fanned across the tops of his cheeks. Cortland committed every minute detail to memory. When the room brightened as the sun rose, Cortland sucked in a deep and ragged sounding breath. It was over.

He slipped from the bed and dressed as quietly as possible. At the bedroom door, Cortland cast another longing glance toward the bed. Every inch he put between them was torture. Cortland took another breath. Each one hurt like it would be his last.

"I love you," Cortland whispered, because he couldn't live without saying the words aloud just once. "Don't hate me." With that final plea, Cortland walked away from the only thing that mattered. He'd never felt more like a failure in his life.

TWO

A loud knocking pulled Driver from the soundest sleep he'd had in years. His eyes shot open and his gaze landed on the empty mattress beside him. The pain that followed stole his breath. He'd known Cortland would leave. That's why it had taken him hours to fall asleep. Driver wondered how long Cortland had waited after he'd gone to sleep before slipping away. Hours? Seconds?

Driver rolled to his feet and grabbed the closest pair of jeans. He hopped on one foot, pulling on his pants on the way to the door. Without bothering to zip or button them, he threw open the door. Jonah was turned away, as if he'd given up, and meant to leave.

"Jonah," Driver called, stopping him "What's up?" Great. Even his voice sounded rough—like Cortland had ripped out his throat when he'd torn out his heart.

Jonah spun. A bright smile lit his face. His gaze skirted Driver's badly covered body before quickly returning to his face and not budging again. Driver bit back a laugh. He'd tried telling Cortland no one else wanted him. Cort should've been here to witness the dismissal. "I stopped by to see if Sam and you would like to go for a walk."

Driver waved Jonah inside. "Sure. Sorry. I'm still waking up." And reeling from Cortland's disappearance. "Let me grab a shirt and Sam's leash."

Jonah led his dog, Cricket inside. The Miniature Schnauzer trotted in the house as if he belonged there. Sam came bounding over, skidding to a stop at the last second. Driver always worried Sam would accidentally kill Cricket, trampling him, but Sam adored the tiny dog. He treated the animal like a baby, licking it and herding him around the living room.

As Driver pulled a shirt over his head, he noticed Jonah looking in every direction. A hint of anxiety set in at Jonah's inspection. He was hyper aware of how bare his home was. Jonah had never been inside before. Driver always managed to stop him at the porch. He recognized his house was nothing like Jonah's—who owned the best of everything. "Have you ever considered a sugar daddy?"

Jonah's question surprised a snort out of Driver. "I'm sorry. What?"

"They have these websites where young guys like us," Jonah said, motioning between them. "Can find older men to keep company in exchange for money. No sex, unless you're looking for that. They just like arm candy for events of whatnot. There's a lot of money in it." He motioned toward Driver's body. "You could easily find someone. I've had the same sugar daddy for a couple of years now. He's pretty awesome. You should have dinner with us some night, so you can see it's not so bad. Just some food for thought."

To his surprise, Driver felt his face heat. He knew what he looked like. His body was still in decent shape, considering his years of homelessness, but still. He was by no means a catch. "Um. I'm not sure that's for me, but thanks." Driver didn't want to insult Jonah. It was rare for Driver to like anyone. He liked Jonah. "I'd still love to have dinner with the two of you some night, though. I'm glad you're taken care of. It's just that I'm not overly friendly and I imagine men are looking for someone not like me," Driver finished lamely. He didn't know how to explain that he wasn't nice or sociable or particularly fond of ninety-nine-point-nine percent of the population. In truth, Cortland was the only person who looked at him like he wasn't a complete piece of shit—like the rest of the world saw the monster inside him.

Jonah smiled. His expression brightened as if relieved Driver wasn't judging him. "I get it, but I still think you'd really like John. Everyone likes him. He's a bit larger than life, but he does take a little while to get used to if you're uncomfortable around boisterous, unfiltered people."

Driver stooped and clicked Sam's leash in place. "Wyld doesn't bother me and he's pretty damn loud and unfiltered, so I'm sure I can handle it."

"Awesome. I'll set something up," Jonah said, opening the door. Driver stopped beside the open door just long enough to shove his feet in some shoes before following Jonah out. The moment they were side by side on the sidewalk, Jonah struck. "So, that guy who showed up last night..."

Driver kept his gaze locked straight ahead. "What about him?"

Jonah didn't pull any punches. "Well, I mean,

men usually only show up at one in the morning for one reason. We see each other every day and I don't think I know anything personal about you at all. You know I'm bought and paid for now. It seems only fair for me to know at least one personal thing about you."

"His name is Cortland," Driver said before he could take it back. He kind of needed someone to know. "He's incredibly out of my league."

A soft chuckle fell from Jonah's lips. "Yet he still showed up. He must disagree."

"Yet he still snuck away," Driver said, incapable of avoiding the thing that was choking him.

"Ouch." Jonah sounded genuinely sympathetic. "Men do that a lot, in my experience. Something about waking up together just scares the hell out of them."

Driver paused so Sam could sniff some bushes. "Well, I'm a guy, and I've never bailed on anyone in the middle of the night."

"I have." Jonah made the admission so easily it surprised Driver. When he looked at Jonah in disbelief, Jonah shrugged. "It wasn't him." Jonah looked thoughtful for a moment. "Or maybe it was. Hell, I don't know. I liked him a lot, but I always came last to him—like it couldn't have been more apparent I was just a last resort booty call. He'd go out with his friends and then only call me when or if he didn't find someone else. Finally, one night I was watching him sleep and my heart was breaking. I realized I was doing it to myself. He wouldn't have a reason to call me last if I didn't show up every damn time he called. So, I gathered what was left of my pride and walked away." A small smile crossed Jonah's features. "When I got home, I created my profile on the sugar daddy site. I figured, if I can let someone shit stomp my heart and pride for free, I could do it for money."

Driver could see Cortland sneaking away to save himself, but Driver would never use the man for only sex. Even though their situations weren't the same, Driver couldn't let Jonah's heartfelt confession pass without comment. "For what it's worth, you deserve to have someone who doesn't use you, regardless if money is involved. You should be with someone nice who treats you good because they care."

Jonah looked away. He wasn't quick enough to hide his flash of hurt. "I'm not that guy, sweetie."

A wave of sadness washed over Driver. He knew there were couples out there like Micah and Wyld who were insanely happy, but most people weren't. Most people didn't find that perfect, forever love. For

Driver, life seemed such a waste. If no one was ever happy why did anyone ever bother?

"I don't think I'm that guy either," Driver admitted.

Jonah linked arms with him and flashed Driver a bright smile. "I guess it's a good thing we're neighbors then. Neither of us will have to limp very far to get help when life goes to shit as it inevitably does."

That was true. Driver definitely needed a friend who wasn't Cortland, especially since it seemed the man was done with him.

DRIVER MADE it all of twenty-four hours before he went in search of Cortland. He'd paced the floor and fought the urge to text him. Driver had even told himself countless times he'd wait until Cortland texted him first before he made a move. The ball was in Cortland's court. Yeah, fuck that. Driver didn't have that much patience. They needed to talk. There wasn't a bus he could take to Cortland's part of town. Billionaires didn't tend to need public transportation. With no choices left to him, he spent way more money than he could spare by taking a cab.

He'd always found the house where Cortland

lived with Micah and Wyld a bit intimidating. It was massive. The place had to be at least seventeen thousand square feet with three floors. Driver hadn't seen much of the inside. What he had seen had been unbelievable. Seeing the place again, after the night he shared with Cortland, only emphasized how out of his league Cortland truly was. It didn't matter the house belonged to Wyld. Cortland was still a part of this world. That knowledge didn't stop Driver's feet from moving for the door. He also didn't hesitate to ring the doorbell. Driver held his breath as he waited. He was scared of how he might react when Cortland opened the door. The desperation inside him could possibly burst from him in any form. As the door swung wide, Driver found himself staring at someone he'd never seen before. For a moment, Driver was thrown for a loop. The large, blond man with light blue eyes didn't look like he fit the place. Driver blinked at the unfamiliar man, trying to decide what to do. Actually, he thought he might have seen him somewhere before, but he couldn't place the guy.

"Did you need something?" The blond asked, obviously losing patience with Driver's frozen brain.

"Sorry. I'm looking for Cortland. He usually answers the door."

"I believe he left for the summer with Wyld and Micah."

"For the summer," Driver repeated. He couldn't believe his ears. Cortland had left. For the whole fucking summer.

The man held his hand out for Driver. "I don't believe we've met. I'm Micah's dad, Payne. They asked me to house sit for them since Cortland wouldn't be here to oversee the place."

"Driver," Driver said, accepting his handshake.

Payne snapped his fingers. "I know the name. You're helping Micah run his tiny home foundation thing, right?"

Driver nodded absently. He was still reeling from the Cortland news. "Yeah. Um, sorry. I took a cab over, expecting Cortland to be here. It'll take me a few minutes to get another cab home. So, if you see me hanging out in the drive, that's why."

Payne stepped outside and pulled the door closed behind him. "I can take you."

Driver shook his head. "That's not necessary. I don't live anywhere near here and don't want to put you out."

"You're not," Payne said, waving off Driver's words. "I have to go pick up my husband from the gym anyhow. It's on the opposite side of town. When

28

you rang the bell, I was already headed for the door to go get him. He had a sparring session this morning that should be finishing up soon. Plus, this will give me a chance to get to know you. Micah has nothing but great things to say about you." He waved Driver toward the driveway where a black GMC sat waiting. He kept talking as he unlocked the truck for Driver. "I admit I don't really get into the whole charity work thing like Micah does. He got that from his mother."

"It's not for everyone." Driver slid into the passenger's seat. He waited until Payne was on his way before speaking again. "I live in the Rosewood subdivision off Lincoln."

Payne nodded. "I know where that is. When we get closer, you can point me in the right direction." Payne drummed his thumbs on the steering wheel, making Driver wonder if he was uncomfortable. He didn't look like the kind of man who was ever out of his comfort zone. In fact, if anyone expected him to describe Payne, he'd go as far as to say the man practically dripped sex. It wasn't the type of thing Driver wanted to notice. It was a detail that was too blinding to ignore. Even the smallest of Payne's movements seemed sensual —like they were calculated. "Is it okay if I ask you a question?" Payne asked, pulling Driver from his musings.

"I guess." Even Driver heard the reluctance in his voice, but the man was taking him home and saving him another cab fee he couldn't afford.

Payne glanced over as if checking Driver's expression before going back to watching the road. "You don't have to answer, if I make you uncomfortable. This is the parent in me, being curious about who my son spends his time with. I know he used to go out of his way to find you, back when you were still on the streets. It always made me nervous for all the obvious reasons."

"You shouldn't worry about Micah," Driver said, cutting in. "Every homeless person in the city knows him and keeps a special watch over him. They all think he's an angel in disguise. I don't know a single person, even the worst of drug addicts, who would let anything happen to him."

Payne flashed him a smile. "I'm not all that surprised. He's always been unique, but still. His stories about you have made curious to know more. There seems to be something about you that made it impossible for my son to let you miss a single meal delivery. And now, he's gone above and beyond to ensure you have a job and a home. I know he'd do the same for anyone. That's who he is, but it's made me super curious about your story. How does someone go from being a sniper for the military to living on the street?"

Payne's question shook Driver a little. He hadn't expected the man to know even that much about him. As much as he didn't want to answer, he could understand Payne wanting to know more about someone who spent so much time with his son. It would make sense Payne would want to know Micah was safe with him. In spite of all the terrible things he'd done, and Payne's deeply personal question, a smile still touched his lips. No one had the courage to ask him what Payne had. He had to respect the man's nerve.

"I'm going to go out on a limb, and guess you've never killed anyone before, much less several someones."

With his eyes locked on the road, Payne nodded. "You'd be right."

Driver swallowed. He had counseling twice a week, but this was different. It was hard to explain something to someone they couldn't possibly fathom. "When I enlisted, I was young and dumb. I thought I could do anything no regrets. It's nowhere near as easy to live with yourself when you're ordered to kill women and children, because they're every bit as big of a threat as the armed men hiding behind them. Long story short, I came home a fucked-up mess." Rage built in his heart every time Driver thought about the red tape he'd run into when he'd come home. It wasn't that he hadn't sought help. No one helped him. "There's endless money to supply weapons to the military, but zero funds to help the people holding those guns when they come home. Possibly, throwing all the money in the world at my mental health wouldn't have helped. Either way, I couldn't function to hold down a job and no one would help me adjust. One day, I no longer cared if I had a roof or lived at all. Until the day Cortland and Micah gave me something to live for again." Now, Cortland had disappeared without a single word of goodbye. Driver didn't know how to feel. He didn't think hurt covered the darkness pressing on his brain and chest. The worst part was, he'd agreed to a single night. He couldn't claim he'd been abandoned. Driver was completely helpless to do anything about it. He could only hope the darkness didn't beat him again.

"I'm glad we talked," Payne said, saving him from the brink of insanity. "Obviously, I'm always proud of my son, but this shows me a side I hadn't considered."

Driver nodded. He had nothing to add. Payne should be proud of Micah. He'd raised an amazing man. Now, that amazing man was out there somewhere with the other half of Driver's soul in tow. Driver didn't know if he'd survive it.

THREE

Tossing and turning all night hadn't done wonders for Driver's mood. He downed some coffee, hoping it would clear his head. Nothing worked. It was a three-block walk to the nearest bus stop to get to work. Driver stamped into his shoes, determined to start out early. He couldn't sit around alone with his thoughts any longer. As he pulled open the door, a box and envelope fell inside the entryway. For a moment, Driver stared down at the items. It wasn't time for the mail. That didn't run until late in the afternoon in his neighborhood. No one had knocked on the door. He picked up the two items and closed the door. Neither the box nor the envelope was marked in any way other than with his name and address. There wasn't any postage or a return address.

Driver opened the letter first.

DRIVER,

I know it's driven into people's head since childhood to open cards and letters first but stop reading and open your gift or this letter won't make sense.

WITH A CHUCKLE, Driver set the letter aside and pulled a knife from his pocket. He couldn't stop smiling. Seeing Cort's handwriting had done wonders for his spirit. He carefully slit the box open, hoping not to ruin whatever was inside. When he upended the container, an eighteen by twenty-four-inch framed sketch slid out. Driver held it up to inspect it. It looked exactly like Cortland from the back, dragging two suitcases and wearing a backpack. The image spoke to Driver on so many levels. It was like he was watching Cortland run away from him. He set the frame aside and picked up the letter.

DID YOU OPEN IT? If so, I'm sorry it's not great. This is the first time I've sketched anything from guessing at it rather than studying it. Plus, it was a rush job. I didn't want you waiting to hear from me forever.

WAIT. Cortland had drawn this? Driver eyed the image once more. Sure enough, Cortland's signature was scrawled in the corner. Impressed, Driver went back to reading.

I KNOW I only asked for one night, so I shouldn't have written, but I'm not good at letting people go. Obviously, or I wouldn't have spent so many years living with Wyld. Joking. He's a good man. Now that he has Micah around, I'm not needed as much. Plus, I have a ton of vacation time built up, so I decided to cash it in while Wyld's traveling the country. Micah's charity runs perfectly in your care and I'm not really needed anywhere anymore. I'm sure you've gathered I'm rambling at this point to avoid saying I'm sorry for sneaking away. Please don't be mad at me. I'll keep in touch.

Hugs, Cort

DRIVER READ and re-read the letter several times. It wasn't a love letter, per se, but Cort had admitted to having a hard time letting Driver go. For now, it would have to be enough. They'd see each other again. He hadn't left with Wyld and Micah, but that was okay. Cortland should get the chance to spend some time traveling without looking back. Driver had agreed to only one night. Just because he intended to make it more didn't mean Cortland had to fall in line. Driver took exception to the part about Cortland not being needed by anyone, but Driver could say that the next time he saw Cortland. They were okay. He hadn't been abandoned. Driver would get his chance to convince Cortland to keep him when Cortland got back.

He turned in a circle, eyeing his bare walls. Driver wanted Cort's picture somewhere he could stare at him all the time. He headed for the bedroom. The spot across from the bed seemed the perfect place to him. That way, Driver could fall asleep every night with Cortland as his last sight. He hadn't known Cortland could draw. Driver kind of liked the idea that he still had new things to discover about the man who'd stolen him. Eventually, he'd uncover every single one of Cort's secrets. Until then, he fucking loved his gift.

THE SECOND LETTER came a week later with another sketch. This time, Driver found a spot for the picture of a corner market in the living room. The third letter arrived three days after the second.

DRIVER,

I'M sure this time around you opened the box first. I can see this tree from my hotel window. It reminds me of you. Even though it doesn't match its surroundings, it's thriving. It looks strong just like you. At least, that's how I see you. You have no idea how much I gravitate toward that strength.

I'll never forget the first time I stumbled into your camp. Micah had made me promise I wouldn't let you avoid getting your meals from the mission. When

Sam bit me, I was certain I'd end up with rabies. After fussing at me for barging into your camp, you cleaned off a spot for me to sit and took care of me. I couldn't look away from your expression. You looked steady. In control. No one has taken care of me in any way in so many years I can't remember. I spend my time in the company of some of the richest people in the world. You had nothing and gave me more.

It's harder than I realized it would be, not talking to you every day. I've never missed someone so much. You can text me if you want. I don't know if I'll have service where I'm at next, but I'll see your messages, eventually. For now, this is all I have. I won't blame you if you decide not to talk to me again. Either way, you'll never hear me say our one night together was a mistake. But it is killing me because I know I have to find a way to go back to how we were before. I'm sorry, Driver. I can't lie to myself or you. No matter what, whether we're friends or more, you'll always be the best part of my life.

Hugs, Cort

THE FOURTH LETTER CAME, but no drawings

accompanied it this time. Instead, Driver had a bigger surprise.

DRIVER,

I promise I'm working on a new sketch for you, but I didn't want to bombard you. What you need more than art for your walls is furniture. Don't be mad. I attended an estate sale yesterday. All the proceeds went to help service members and veterans suffering from PTSD. I might've gotten a little carried away, but it was for a good cause. One I knew you could get behind. A delivery man will be there Thursday afternoon after four with your stuff. I know you don't like to accept help. Please don't turn my gift away. Tell yourself you're doing your part to help a good cause, if you need to. After all, I don't have any use for any more furniture and the money went to help people. As I said, I know you don't like it, but I need to do this because I care. A lot. Do this for me.

Hugs, Cort

CORTLAND HAD DONE TOO MUCH. He

filled Driver's house with furniture. If Cortland had been around for Driver to balk, he would have. It wasn't just any old furniture either. Each piece was beautiful and obviously expensive. Cortland had also bought him all new electronics, including flat screen TVs for his living room, bedroom, and even a small one for the corner of his kitchen. While he'd been dealing with the delivery of a shit ton of new furniture, a tech had shown up to install his new satellite. Driver had tried turning the guy away until he'd been informed the entire system and a year-long subscription had already been paid in full. No refunds allowed.

Driver dragged his fingers through his hair in frustration again just thinking about it. He didn't know how to deal with someone forcing this much materialistic stuff upon him, especially when that person was god only knows where. At least a fucking car hadn't magically appeared in his driveway. At the rate things were going, Driver wouldn't be surprised. Letters and framed sketches kept coming though. Every few days or weeks a new delivery would arrive. They came via a private delivery company. Driver only knew because he'd stalked the fucking deliveries like an insane person. There was only one thought keeping him sane—the summer was almost over. Cortland had to come home soon, right?

THE VIEW WAS beautiful from Cortland's room. He'd been inspired to draw like he hadn't been in years in the last couple of months. Cortland didn't know if it was the view or Driver that truly stirred him. Either way, he'd seen things differently the past months. Missing Driver was killing him a little more every day. He'd been celibate for several years before Driver. It was partially by choice and mostly due to trauma. Now, his body burned for Driver all hours of the day.

He picked up his sketchpad and eyed the half-finished drawing of a nearby park bench. It was missing something. With a growl, Cortland tossed it aside and grabbed his notebook instead. Maybe if he wrote another letter to Driver, he'd see what he'd missed.

DRIVER,

DAMN. Just seeing the man's name set Cortland's body ablaze. He could picture Driver's piercing blue eyes and fierce stare like the man was in the room. Cortland sucked in a ragged sounding breath. The image of Driver's gaze locked on his as he'd pumped inside him... damn. Cortland's chest felt heavy at the memory. He blinked, focusing on his task.

THERE'S a park bench outside one of my windows. It's cemented into the sidewalk, as if built for those waiting for the next bus to arrive. The thing that baffles me is, it's facing away from the street. I stared at it for nearly an hour the other day, trying to decide why it's there. I'm sending you a sketch, so you can help me decide. It's facing a hill. I guess I might understand if there was a park or even an empty field within view, but no. There's a road, the park bench, and then a grassy hill—completely in that order. It's part of the sidewalk. There's no chance someone physically moved it from a park to there. Its placement was intentional on someone's part. The most logical conclusion is that someone fucked up, but I get bored and stories about this bench pop into my head. I won't bore you with those.

Whatever the reason for its location, it has to be

the most popular bench on the planet. People come and go all day. Even though the bench is in full view of the world, something about the fact that it faces the wrong way must make people feel invisible. I've seen some things happen on that bench. Things I can't unsee.

CORTLAND RUBBED HIS CHEST. The aching heaviness increased.

FUCK, I miss you.

CORTLAND PAUSED. He almost scratched through the words. They were unfair. He'd only asked for one night. He shouldn't say things like that. Cortland couldn't stop.

JUST ONE MORE TIME, I'll pour out my heart. I'm sorry. I get that I keep saying that. Maybe I can't stop. What will happen to our friendship if I can't? When you see me next, you can act like you didn't read this letter. I'll pretend I didn't write it. You are *easily the most gorgeous man I've ever met. I know there's nothing special about that compliment. Anyone with eyes and a tongue can tell you that, but I see you from the inside out. I know sometimes you scare yourself. All the over-the-top reactions you have that terrify you make me feel safe. They make me feel desired. I wish you were here right now.*

CORTLAND STARED AT NOTHING. The world fell away. He was back in that shower with Driver. Driver had just dipped his head beneath the water to rinse his hair. His sexy full lips called Cortland's name. The way the water streamed down Driver's gorgeous body, parting as it reached his erection made Cortland's mouth water. He'd been incapable of resisting and lunged forward. Cortland touched his lips. He could still feel that kiss. Unexpectedly, Cortland's eyes burned with unshed tears. His throat swelled. He hadn't anticipated missing Driver this much. They couldn't go back to being just friends. Maybe Driver could, but Cortland couldn't. Goddamn, he ached. His heart was missing. It was trapped with Driver and Cortland didn't think he'd ever get it back again. Panic rose. His mind was stuck in a destructive cycle. He needed Driver. His phone buzzed, shocking a gasp from him. He thought his eardrums might explode from the sound after being trapped in silence for so long. Driver's name appeared on the face of Cortland's phone. Air inflated his lungs. Calm settled over him. His heart wasn't so far away after all.

———

DRIVER'S MIND wandered as he made his usual trip to the bus stop. He needed to grab Sam some food while he was out. Cortland had sent him another letter this morning. Driver kept trying to think of something else, but Cortland had said a lot in his last letter. Driver had never wanted to kick time in the ass to get it moving so bad in his life. Cortland had said he missed Driver. Driver had felt those words as he'd read them. The hope building inside him was half terror and half madness. Until Cortland came home, Driver didn't know which side he'd land on.

The bookstore window caught his eye as he passed. He hadn't bought a new book in a while. There was a used bookstore two blocks over that was a better fit for his budget. As the item in the window penetrated his wayward thoughts, Driver's feet froze and refused to budge. Thankfully, there wasn't anyone on his heels or they would've crashed into him. A familiar scrawled signature caught and held his attention. In the window of a bookstore, just a short walk from his house, Driver stared at a piece of Cortland. A large leather-bound book stood open on a stand, showing sketches of a cabin on a lake and one of an empty field. Driver swallowed. They were Cortland's. He'd recognize Cort's signature anywhere.

Driver headed inside. He needed a closer look. The scent of new books washed over him as he stepped through the door. *Gah.* He could feel his wallet getting lighter already. The window display was blocked off, forcing Driver to hunt down an employee. He spotted an older lady dusting shelves nearby.

"Excuse me. Are there any more copies of the book you have in the window?"

The woman pushed her salt and pepper hair out of her face as she turned Driver's way. She smiled, obviously excited about the topic. "The Cortland Fletcher collection? Sure. We have a few. Well, more than a few," she said, sounding guilty as she waved him down the aisle. "In truth, I ordered too many. He's a local, you know? I'd hoped to convince him to do a signing. It would've been a huge boon for business, but he declined." She happily chattered along, and Driver hung on every word. Cortland didn't feel as far away with someone talking about him. "I'm honestly not surprised he turned me down though. Such a sad story on that one."

"A sad story?" Driver repeated hoping to keep her talking.

She pulled a leather-bound book from the shelf and passed it his way. "I guess a lot of artists come from tragic backgrounds. You hear the heartbreaking stories over and over about authors, artists, and poets. Pain breeds beauty, I suppose."

Driver nodded toward the book he held. He tried to sound interested but not too interested. Driver needed her to keep talking. "What's this artist's story?"

It was obvious the woman relished an audience. Her smile screamed that she knew all the gossip. "Well, like a lot of artists, he's gay."

Driver ground his back teeth. The need to learn all there was to know about Cortland outweighed his desire to point out how she was stereotyping. After all, he was gay too, and he didn't have an artistic bone in his body.

"His parents were convinced their son would go

to hell and take them with him if they stood by and did nothing." She pressed her hand to her stomach, as if it churned at the idea of speaking her next words, but she didn't stop. "They hired some men who supposedly had great results with conversion therapy and sent him away with them." Driver went cold. Unfortunately, she didn't stop. "It turned out, these men's methods were even worse than the usual horrors you hear about. They believed, if they took turns gang raping the boys in their care, they would realize they didn't enjoy sex and turn to the lord." Driver couldn't breathe well enough to tell her to stop. "When his parents realized even extreme measures didn't make him less feminine, they turned him out into the streets, so he wouldn't taint their souls. Now, I hear he suffers from a bit of Haphephobia, stemming from the abuse." She ran her hand over the outside of the book Driver held, obviously moved by someone she'd never personally met. "It doesn't make things better, but he persevered, and his work means something to people now."

Driver fought the urge to hug the book to his chest because he couldn't hold Cortland. He cleared his throat, trying to find his voice. "I'm sorry, but what is Haphephobia?"

She pressed her hands to her cheeks as if embarrassed by not realizing he might not know what she meant. "Oh, sorry. It's a paralyzing aversion to being touched—like it can be so bad that even the smallest brush of skin is extremely painful. They say he doesn't go out much, or if he does, he goes places he's not likely to be forced to shake hands with strangers, bump into people, or anything like that. Otherwise, he has to be heavily medicated. I can't imagine living like that. It must be really lonely."

Driver dropped his gaze to the book he held to hide his reaction. Yes, he got the impression Cortland was very lonely. "How much is this?" he asked, trying to keep a tight hold on his sanity.

"Two hundred."

If it had been any other book, it would've gone straight back on the shelf. Driver would have to pull from his tiny savings for this one, but Cortland's book was coming home with him. "Okay. I'll get it." He tried not to choke on the words. It looked like it would be another few months before he got that used truck he'd been eyeing. Cortland was worth it. Driver felt closer to Cortland just holding his work. Damn, sometimes it felt like they'd never see each other again. Never before had he wished harder that life was different. That he could afford to hunt

Cortland down and try to fix what he could. Even though it was obvious Cortland's story was either common knowledge or a computer click away, Driver felt like Cortland had done nothing but keep secrets. No one had ever made him feel more helpless, and that was saying a lot.

FOUR

In all honesty, Driver hadn't known what to expect when it came to meeting Jonah's man. He couldn't avoid going to dinner with them forever. But each time Jonah talked about the whole sugar daddy thing, he pictured some ridiculously old man with one foot in the grave and dragging the other with a cane while parading Jonah around town, bragging to his elderly friends. As he opened the door to the pair, he realized he'd been wrong. Very wrong. John was closer to Cortland's age. Not only was the man in good health, he appeared to be the epitome of manliness. The dude was like a mountain. If mountains were made of muscle, that is. He had dark hair and sweet brown eyes. His smile was bright and contagious. Before John even opened his mouth, Driver found himself smiling, and he had no idea why.

"Driver," John boomed, sounding every bit as big as he was. "I've heard so much about you."

Driver wasn't much of a smiler. His cheeks already hurt. "You as well. Come in." He took a step back, waving the pair inside.

Jonah kept switching his gaze between them, openly expectant—like he'd just introduced his two favorite people. With John there, Jonah didn't get a chance to speak.

"Jonah says I'm not supposed to point out the fact that your place is sparse, but it doesn't look that way to me."

Jonah covered his eyes, looking horrified.

A laugh sneaked its way out. "In his defense, I've gotten some new furniture since the last time he was here."

John's gaze locked on a spot over Driver's shoulder. "Holy shit. You own an original Cortland Fletcher." His gaze moved down the line of frames. "Damn. You have more than one. That's amazing." John stepped around Driver and eyed Cortland's sketches, making himself at home. "How did you get these? How much do you want for them? I'll give you ten thousand for this one," he said, pointing at the image of the park bench Cortland had drawn for him.

"It's not for sale." Driver didn't mean to sound quite so gruff when he answered but the pictures meant everything to him.

John nodded and went back to staring at the sketch. "You're right. It's worth more than ten. How about thirty?"

Driver shook his head. "You don't understand. They're priceless to me."

"Damn, boy. You drive a hard bargain. The highest I can go is fifty."

"They're not—"

"Give us a minute, babe," Jonah said, talking over the top of Driver. "Let me deal for you."

John smiled and headed for the door. "I'll be right outside, sexy. If you manage to get a deal for me, I'll make it worth your while."

Jonah winked as John passed. Driver wanted to scream. No one ever listened to him. He couldn't sell Cortland's drawings. The moment they were alone, Driver exploded. "I can't sell Cortland's sketches. They're all I have left of him."

Jonah held up his hands in a calming gesture. "Just hear me out. John loves to throw his money around. Pick one, sell it to him, and use the money to go see the real Cortland. Selling just one could make the difference in winning your man. Imagine his face if you turned up at his door."

"The summer is almost over. Surely, he'll be home soon. Plus, I can't just go after him. Cort left for a reason. Granted, I don't really know what that reason is, but still. I don't think I should chase him down. He might not take it well. I don't want to fuck things up."

Jonah's eyebrows rose, as if daring Driver to man up. "I disagree. You most certainly can take John's money and go. Cortland already left, Driver. What's the worst that could happen by taking a risk? Men like men who seize the day."

Driver licked his suddenly parched lips. Before this moment, he hadn't thought he had any chance of seeing Cortland until Cortland got tired of traveling and came home. There was a risk involved despite what Jonah thought. "He could stop writing me. If I chase him, he might disappear for good and not look back." That was one outcome Driver couldn't live with.

"Or he could finally realize how much you really care and stop running. The fact is, you won't know until you try. At least think about it, or say you'll think about it anyhow. That'll keep John happy tonight. Otherwise, you'll never hear the end of it. Trust me, I once said we could skip an expensive trip and just stay at my place for the weekend. Jesus, it was the longest four hours of my life until I gave in."

Driver chuckled. He could picture John being a bulldog when he wanted his way. "Fine. Tell him I'll think about it."

The way Jonah's shoulders sagged with relief let Driver know he'd made the right choice. "Come on. Let's get out of here before he finds a priceless antique chair on your porch or some shit."

With a nod, Driver headed for the door. When they stepped outside, John's face lit. He looked so hopeful, Driver almost said yes just to make him smile. "I'll think about it and let you know in the next few weeks."

John nodded. "Smart move. Have them appraised first. You don't want to get taken for a ride." Driver shook his head. He'd never met anyone like John. He got the feeling it was impossible to dislike the man. "Let's eat. I'm starving," John said, linking fingers with Jonah and heading for a giant red

Hummer sitting at the curb. Driver followed on their heels, hanging back while trying to stay out of the way. John was having no part of it. After he opened the passenger side door for Jonah, he held the back door open for Driver. Even though Driver was as uncomfortable as could be, he still nodded his thanks and climbed in. The minute John was behind the wheel, he regaled them with stories about his day, but he jumped topics so fast Driver couldn't keep up. Jonah seemed to follow just fine, popping in with several questions about people Driver didn't know until Driver lost interest and stared out the window. The longer they drove, the more upscale the properties became until Driver no longer recognized his surroundings. There wasn't a single piece of shit car in sight and everything looked polished.

"Whoops," John boomed, making Driver jump and pulling his attention John's way. "I almost forgot I need to make a stop." He pulled to the shoulder of the road without further explanation. As Driver looked on, John jumped from the vehicle and darted across the street to a small market while dodging cars along the way.

"What the hell?" Driver muttered under his breath.

A chuckle rumbled from the front seat. "That's

John for you. He had a whim. All we can do is wait to see what it is."

Driver found himself staring at the market, oddly curious. Something niggled at Driver's thoughts. There was something about the place. Driver's mind went on high alert. He damn near snapped his fingers in an ah-ha moment. It was the corner market from Cortland's sketch. He twisted in his seat, eyeing their surroundings. Behind them sat the park bench. Sure enough, it was cemented into the sidewalk and faced a hill. Across the street, Cortland's tree. Every sketch Cortland sent him was from this spot. There was only one place in full view of each location from the sketches. It was a business set off the road. Driver didn't see a sign or anything else that would give him a hint to what the place was.

The driver's side door opened, and John jumped inside. He handed Jonah a huge bouquet of red roses. "For you, sexy angel."

"Awww," Jonah cooed, sounding genuinely happy. He brought the flowers to his nose and sniffed. A half second before the roses hid his expression, Driver caught a glimpse of Jonah's heart. He could accept all the gifts and money, telling himself this was a business transaction he could walk away from at any moment, but Driver had seen the truth. John owned Jonah in every way, including the man's heart. Driver looked away. There was no scenario where Jonah didn't get hurt. He was John's possession. Nothing more.

"I didn't forget about you," John said, pulling Driver's attention back their way. "You don't strike me as the flower type, but I can't take you out and not buy you a gift. Here." He passed a paper bag to Driver.

Even though he didn't want to accept, Driver already knew John would be insulted if he didn't. Driver glanced inside the bag. Against his will, a smile tugged at the corners of his mouth. There were two books inside. Both were newly released, and both were by his favorite authors. The man was good. Driver couldn't deny it.

Driver met John's expectant gaze. "Thank you. This is truly amazing. It's like you read my mind."

A boisterous laugh filled the car, making Driver's smile grow. John was loud and overwhelming, but in a good way. It was obvious he had a kind heart. "I'm observant. Now, are you two ready to be blown away? I'm telling you, this new restaurant is amazing."

"Beyond ready," Jonah said, sounding happy.

Driver's gaze slid back toward the anonymous

building. "Do either of you know what that place is?" he asked rather than answering John's question.

Both men peered out the window. John was the one who answered. "It's one of those super exclusive hotel and spas for the rich. You know, where they get mental health treatment under the guise of relaxing. There're only about twenty rooms but each room has a pool cave inside, so you can even swim in privacy. It's pretty sweet. The pool looks out over the bluffs, so there's no chance of anyone disturbing you." He focused on Jonah. "There's another place like that in San Diego that isn't for only health purposes. It's perfect for romantic getaways. We should go there some weekend."

"I'd love that."

John winked at Jonah's open willingness to do whatever John suggested before pulling away from the curb. Driver focused on the building once more, staring until he could no longer see it. His mind didn't want to accept what his heart already knew. Cortland hadn't gone anywhere. He was still here, right beneath Driver's nose... falling apart. Every letter Cortland sent, a lie. The furniture he'd received, probably new and ordered online. Driver took a breath. His chest hurt. The SUV he occupied was headed away from his heart. It had been one thing to believe Cortland was out there somewhere, traveling the country and enjoying a much-needed vacation. It was another to know Cortland was right there, seeking solace because he'd touched Driver. Nothing had changed. Driver was still poison, killing everything beautiful he encountered.

FIVE

With the summer months drawing to an end, Cortland would have to go home soon. Not much would change when he got there, besides returning to running Wyld and Micah's household, but he wouldn't be able to avoid Driver. With Driver working for Micah's charity, they'd be back to seeing each other daily. There was no way around it. Cortland loved Wyld too much to abandon him and Driver was too good at connecting with the homeless on a personal level to lose him. Cortland just needed to harden his heart against the idea of Driver. He loved Driver. That meant he owed Driver a better life than Cortland could give him. Driver deserved all the affection Cortland didn't know how to show. All Cortland had was the ability to buy him whatever he wanted and these sketches.

He shaded a spot beneath the palm tree, perfectly matching the one hanging over the edge of the pool. He was almost finished, and then he'd send this new piece Driver's way along with his latest letter. The hotel staff had gotten really good at having his drawings framed and delivered. Cortland knew he could call Driver anytime he liked, but Cortland was too weak. All it would take was one word from Driver's lips and Cortland would be begging for another night. And then another. That wasn't fair to Driver. Cortland glanced up from his sketchbook for one final check of the details. His gaze landed on the sexiest sight in the world. He blinked. Driver was still there. Cortland's mouth went dry. "How did you get in here?" Even he didn't understand why that was his first thought. It should've been something better. Something welcoming, but seriously. Cortland was sitting on a lounge chair inside the pool cave in his room, completely out of sight and reach. Yet, here Driver was, looking as if he'd waltzed in.

Driver's mouth lifted in one corner. "I've worked undercover dark ops for our country. A spa on American soil is nothing."

"You're here." Cortland didn't know why he couldn't stop pointing out the obvious. He was ecstatic. Truly, he was. His mouth just wouldn't get onboard. Too many times to count he'd wondered how he'd react the next time he saw Driver. Now that moment was here before Cortland expected it, and he wanted more, just as he feared he would.

Driver sat on the edge of Cortland's lounge chair. Their hips almost touched. He could feel the heat radiating from Driver's skin. "You led me to believe you were traveling."

Cortland dropped his gaze to his book. "This is as close as I get to traveling. Maybe one day." He shaded an area with his finger, smearing the chalk. Cortland turned the pad for Driver to see. "This was my next delivery to you."

Driver took the sketch and looked it over. His expression didn't give anything away. "It's beautiful." He handed it back. "Since you're not really traveling, I guess it's safe to assume my furniture didn't come from an estate sale as you claimed."

If Driver wanted to discuss furniture rather than Cortland's sneaking away for a summer-long stint in a mental health facility, Cortland was fine with that. "It's new," Cortland admitted. "However," he added before Driver lost his shit. "I did bid for it online and the profits went to a charity to help soldiers with PTSD. That part wasn't a lie."

Driver's gorgeous blue gaze moved over Cortland's face. "You're amazing, you know? If you'd stuck around, I would've told you that every day."

There it was. The reason he couldn't get enough. A sad smile pulled at Cortland's lips. "I'm really not, though."

It was like Driver wasn't hearing him. "Will you kick me out if I kiss you?"

The longing that hit Cortland nearly felled him. He tried to find some humor in the situation to hide the pain. "No. As much as I'm paying to be here, I can do what I please."

Driver looked away. A sad smile crossed his features as he stared at something in the distance. "You wouldn't let me, so it's a moot point."

Cortland's hand lifted. The need to touch Driver was a fire in his blood, burning him alive. At the last second, he dropped his hand and toyed with the string of his swim trunks instead. If Driver was here, that meant he knew what this place was, and—most likely—why Cortland was here. "I wanted to be better for you." He took a breath. It sounded louder and more ragged than he expected. "For a long time, I thought I'd found peace, living virtually alone in

Wyld's huge house and semi-functioning on a normal level. Then I met you and I realized I'm not better. I'm hiding."

Driver glanced over. He snagged the end of the string Cortland held. They each twisted until they almost touched. It was like they were holding hands and Cortland felt it in his chest.

"You deserve someone better," Cortland whispered past his rapidly swelling throat.

After dropping the string, Driver looked away again and visibly swallowed. "So I made you worse." A humorless smile touched his lips before disappearing. "That sounds about right." Driver stood. "After spotting the bench from your letter, I just needed to see for myself that you were really here." Cortland's eyes fell closed for a moment. Of course, that damn bench had given him away. Even though Driver faced Cortland, his gaze didn't drop to Cortland's face. Instead he stared at some point over Cortland's head. "Whenever you're ready to leave here, you don't have to worry about seeing me. I don't need a job so badly I'd hurt the only person I love to keep it."

"Driver, no," Cortland begged, feeling like the lowest of scum while still reeling from Driver's L-bomb. "You do need your job."

"Just work on feeling whole again," Driver said, speaking over the top of him. "You don't have to worry about me anymore." Driver walked away, tearing out Cortland's heart as he went.

Cortland stared at the pool, seeing nothing. He wanted to chase after Driver. His feet wouldn't budge. He wanted to scream. His throat wouldn't work. Cortland swallowed. "I was never whole," he whispered too late for Driver to hear. That was his life though, wasn't it? He was always a second too late to save himself from the worst possible scenario. Cortland should've seen this coming.

HE HAD TO GET OUT. That was the only thought in Driver's head. Everything he'd done in the past several months, he'd done for Cortland. He appreciated Micah and Wyld. They'd given him a new life. Without Cortland having given him a reason to fight, he never would've accepted Micah's job offer. Having four walls and ceiling surrounding him only created another house to trap his horrible thoughts. He had to get out before he did any more damage. All Driver did was destroy everything, especially the people he loved.

His crazed thoughts carried him across the street the moment he made it home. When Jonah answered, Driver jumped in with both feet like the crazy person he was. He couldn't give himself time to think. Driver was weak when it came to Cortland. "Do you think John would still want to buy Cortland's sketches?"

Jonah blinked at Driver as if overwhelmed by his burst of words with no hello. "I'm sure he would. How many do you have?"

"Ten." Minus the one of Cortland in Driver's bedroom. He could never part with that one.

Jonah waved him inside. "Come in and I'll text him. He's always pretty quick to text me back. You look impatient to be rid of them."

Guilt weighed more than Driver expected. "I need the money."

A bright smile lit Jonah's face. His gaze lifted from his phone to meet Driver's. "Are you finally going after Cortland?"

"No. I'm finally getting out of his way."

Jonah's smile fell. He sat. "Oh, sweetie. What happened?"

Pain washed over Driver, swelling his throat. He tried to speak. No words came. He knew he'd break if he explained. Someone who'd stolen so much life didn't get to move on and be happy. For the rest of his life, Driver would pay for his actions. Whereas most killers spent their lives behind bars, paying for their crime, Driver had to spend the rest of his life inside the prison in his head. He'd known he didn't deserve happiness when he met Cortland. Driver had never meant to drag Cortland into his hell. Cortland didn't deserve to have anything else happen to him. He deserved peace. Driver would give it to him. None of those confessions would make their way to Driver's lips.

"He never left so I have to."

Jonah visibly floundered. His mouth opened as if to speak before snapping closed again. He blinked and tried again. "What do you mean he never left? Like, he never left town?"

Driver nodded. That was all the strength he had.

Anger flashed in Jonah's eyes. "Has he just been hiding from you this whole goddamn time while you were sitting around, worrying and waiting?"

Hurt wouldn't release its hold on Driver's tongue. He nodded again.

"Well, fuck that." Jonah dropped his gaze to his phone and furiously typed. The phone dinged, and Jonah kept typing. He'd never seen anyone fire off texts so fast. A satisfied looking smile stretched

Jonah's lips. He met Driver's stare, looking proud of himself. "John says he'll give you two hundred thousand for all ten if he can give you a hundred thousand by the end of the day and the other half by the end of tomorrow."

Driver's guilt doubled. The deep sense of loss over selling Cortland's sketches was four times as heavy as the guilt. He nodded. "That's fine." His eyes fell closed even as he agreed to John's terms. Cortland was gone from his life for good now. All that was left to do was leave. Driver had no idea where he was headed. All he knew was he couldn't stay here.

CORTLAND STARED at his bedroom ceiling, trying to decide what to do. Should he go straight to Driver and beg for him to understand or explain? He'd been home for less than an hour. No matter how many times he went over things in his head, he couldn't figure out where he'd gone wrong. That wasn't true. He shouldn't have sneaked away. Cortland should've woken Driver, confessed everything, and then gone for the help he needed. The thing was, he didn't want Driver to see him as broken, even though he was. How fucked up was that? It was a vicious cycle that was breaking him. His phone buzzed, crawling across his stomach where he'd left it sitting, while he debated on calling Driver. Cortland snatched it up, praying to see Driver's name.

Micah: *I know you're on vacation, but we have a code red emergency. Driver quit. No notice. He's just gone.*

Cortland: *I got home this morning. I'll start looking for a replacement.*

Micah: *I'm on my way home now too, but what about Driver? I don't want a replacement. We need Driver. Did he say anything to you? Why would he quit? Is he backsliding in his counseling sessions? I don't understand what's happening.*

Cortland: *I'll look into everything. Don't panic yet.*

Micah: *I'm trying. I'll be home in two hours. Keep me posted.*

Cortland dropped the phone and covered his face with his hands. All of this was his fault. It was like, if he ever felt anything about anyone, his life fell apart. If he could've been born straight, he never would've lost his parents. A lot of things would've never happened if he could've been different. Now, for the first time, he'd fallen in love and he destroyed that person too. He didn't know how to make anyone happy, least of all himself.

Cortland's hands fell to his lap. He would fix this. If anyone lost their job, it would be him. He'd hoped, with a little of counseling, he'd find a way to be with Driver. All that happened was he'd hurt someone he cared about. It didn't matter Driver had agreed to only one night. Cortland had known it wouldn't be that way for either of them. He'd let the lie grow in his heart because he wanted Driver. Cortland had let himself believe Driver would let him go after one night together because he needed to think it was true.

Now, everything was a mess. Cortland snatched up his phone. He wouldn't be weak. Driver deserved better from him.

Cortland: *You fucking quit? Really? You just fucking quit? I spent the last three months in a treatment program, trying to find a way to be with you, and you just fucking quit. Well, stay gone then.*

Cortland blinked down at the message he'd typed in his rage and it was too late. He'd sent it before his mind cleared. Goddamn it. He fought the urge to chuck the phone across the room. Instead, he turned off the device before he did anything else stupid. Cortland pushed to his feet and gathered his things to leave. Keys and phone in hand, Cortland headed for his car. He tried to keep his mind blank as he drove to Driver's. Cortland didn't have a plan. He didn't know what to say. Hell, he wasn't even sure how to feel. All Cortland knew was, he couldn't let Driver ruin his life over him. Cortland wasn't worth it.

At Driver's, Cortland knew he'd been right to leave immediately. It was obvious Driver was moving out. A truck sat in the driveway, backed up to the front door. The tailgate was down, and boxes filled the back. Driver's front door stood open. Cortland slowly ascended the front steps. Voices filtered outside from the living room. Driver wasn't alone. Cortland hardened his heart against it. He was here for Driver. His jealousy and desires meant nothing. All that mattered was Driver's happiness. He couldn't let the man he loved go back to being jobless and possibly homeless.

As he cleared the doorway, he spotted the young guy who lived across the street. His gaze moved Cortland's way and froze. He snatched up a box and headed for the door. Cortland moved aside to let him pass. It couldn't have been more obvious the guy was making himself scarce.

Driver turned to grab an empty box. His gaze turned hungry as he eyed Cortland, the way it always did. "Did you come to tell me to stay gone in person?"

"I shouldn't have said that," Cortland said, crossing the room. He grabbed an empty box and started loading books inside. Cortland could feel Driver watching him, but he didn't make eye contact. His throat and chest hurt. The backs of his eyes burned. None of that mattered. Driver needed his help.

"Why are you doing this?" Driver asked, breaking the silence.

"Friends help each other move. I'm your friend."

"Is that all I am to you?"

Cortland took a deep breath. He would survive this. Maybe. "No, but it doesn't matter how I feel. I learned a long damn time ago that I'm not good enough to..." Cortland swallowed his words. He wouldn't take the low road. "Never mind." He kept his gaze locked on his hands. "You're obviously set on leaving. I love you too much to hold you back." Cortland crossed the room and grabbed more books. He kept talking as he worked. "All I've ever wanted was for you to be happy."

They worked on packing boxes across from one

another for several minutes before Driver spoke again. "Did I hurt you?"

Cortland glanced up at the question. "What?"

Driver didn't look his way. "That night. Did it hurt when I touched you?"

The air froze in Cortland's lungs. Anger turned his heart to ice. "If you want to leave me, I can't stop you. I'll help you pack and watch you go, even though it's killing me. But I'll be damned if I rip my heart out for inspection for someone who doesn't care enough about me to stay."

"I—"

"No," Cortland said, cutting him off. Rage flooded his system. It didn't matter Cortland didn't want to feel that way. "Maybe I didn't tell you exactly where I went, but I didn't abandon you. You heard from me on a regular basis all summer. I won't apologize for wanting to fix me before I destroyed you. So just fucking go, Driver. No one is stopping you." Cortland wanted to be a friend and help. He couldn't do this. Cortland dropped the books he held in a box and headed for the door. It was better if he left now.

"Cortland."

With his gaze locked on his shoes, Cortland picked up the pace. He didn't look back. His whole life, he'd been awkward and too serious. Cortland had honestly believed Driver understood him—got him on a level no one else ever had. He'd thought Driver knew his hard shell was the only thing holding together the mess inside him. It seemed he was wrong. The guy from across the street who always seemed to be around, still lingered outside. Cortland didn't look his way either. The dark-haired boy was closer to Driver in age. Maybe he could make Driver happy in all the ways Cortland couldn't. Cortland told himself he didn't care. He'd always been a master at lying to himself.

DRIVER FOLLOWED CORTLAND OUTSIDE. Cortland never looked back as he jumped into his car, leaving Driver behind. He watched Cortland go until he couldn't see him anymore. Too many realizations were crashing their way in for him to react as he should.

"What happened?"

At Jonah's question, Driver tore his gaze away from the road and focused on Jonah's face. Everything had a blurry hue. He swallowed past the panic rapidly rising in his throat. "I think I was wrong."

A line appeared between Jonah's brows. "What do you mean?"

"Everything. I was wrong about everything." Driver sucked in a ragged breath. Hyperventilating was right around the corner. "I shouldn't have sold his sketches or quit my job. He deserved better from me. I let all my ideas about not deserving happiness self-destruct what could've been while he worked his ass off to get better. I was wrong, Jonah." He dragged air into his lungs, but no oxygen reached his brain like he was drowning. Even though Driver knew he was having a panic attack, the knowledge didn't slow the growing hysteria over not being able to breathe. "I don't..." Driver sucked more air, trying to keep from fainting, "... know how..." he panted, "... to fix it."

Jonah rushed to his side. He steered him toward the house while rubbing his back. "It's okay. Just breathe. I'll help you. While you call and get your job back, I'll call John and talk to him about the sketches. You'll probably have to let one or two go, since you already spent some of the money. I think I can convince John to give back the rest." Driver hung on every word, hoping against hope that he didn't slip back into that dark place Cortland already saved him from once. "We'll figure this out," Jonah assured him. "I don't think it's too late for you to say you're sorry. It's never too late for that."

Driver nodded even though he wasn't so sure. Cortland had done something for Driver he'd never done for anyone else. He'd risked his heart. Driver had let him down. It might not be as easy as apologizing. Possibly, Driver had ruined the best thing ever to happen to him and there was no taking it back.

SIX

Beads of water rolled down Cortland's body as he left the bathroom. With a towel wrapped around his waist, Cortland headed for the dresser. When he reached the solid oak piece, he stared at it in confusion. He couldn't remember what he'd been doing. Everything hurt too badly. He couldn't function. Cortland braced his palms on the edge of the dresser. His shoulders fell. He stared down at his rapidly whitening knuckles, seeing nothing. There'd been a time when living here, running Wyld's life, had been enough for him. He'd find that place again. No one had broken through his shell before Driver. It wouldn't happen again. Cortland wouldn't allow it. He just needed time to let him go. The counselling he'd received helped. Not that it mattered now. But, maybe he'd leave here and travel for real. Dedicate himself to art.

"I hate knowing I'm the reason you look so tired."

Cortland spun. His heart slammed against the wall of his chest. Driver sat at the end of Cortland's bed. Cortland had no idea how long he'd been there or how he'd gotten in. "Fuck, Driver. How the hell do you keep sneaking into places?"

Driver's serious expression never wavered. "I didn't have to sneak. Micah answered the door. After we talked, he sent me in here. I doubt he realized you were in the shower."

That made sense. Micah knew they were friends. He wouldn't hesitate to send Driver to Cortland's room.

"I'm sorry," Driver added before Cortland could respond. "So fucking sorry. You're the one person I never wanted to fail. The thing is, you're so much stronger than I am. I guess I forgot that you're human too. It never occurred to me that you might need to walk away from me to save yourself. I obviously have some issues." A sad smile touched Driver's lips. "For a little while, you made me feel so much stronger than I am. I almost forgot how fucked in the head I am until you were gone. Then, I questioned everything about myself, and that's not on you." He looked so crestfallen it weighed on Cortland's chest. "I'll never be able to apologize enough."

Cortland leaned back against the dresser and eyed Driver. He hated how upset Driver looked. Cortland wasn't the type of person to make anyone grovel, and he loved Driver too much to want the man to feel bad. He also realized he wasn't guilt free. At the end of the day, Driver was still his best friend. "Do you remember the day we met? When Sam bit me?"

A sexy smile crossed Driver's features. "How could I forget? It's not every day someone storms a homeless camp, wearing thousand-dollar shoes and a ten-thousand-dollar watch." Driver's smile brightened. "You looked enraged you'd been forced to hunt me down, and then my mangy mutt, as you called him, had the audacity to bite you. All because I was being difficult."

Driver's recount forced a chuckle from Cortland. He couldn't deny he'd been annoyed by having to search out Driver. It was possible he came off as a bit haughty that day. "You held my arm as you cleaned the wound," Cortland reminded him of the part he'd left out. "It was the first time anyone had touched me in years where it didn't feel like a hot poker was being taken to my skin." Driver winced at the analogy. Cortland didn't stop. "I don't know if it was because I was pissed off or what, but I think it was just you. From that moment on, every time I saw you, I searched for ways to touch you. So, to answer your question from earlier today, no. You didn't hurt me that night. But I was still scared that I'd wake up one day and that pain would return. I needed to seek the help I was never brave enough to get before you. You matter to me. I don't want to fail you. I sure as hell don't want to trap you with someone who—without warning—can't tolerate your touch any longer."

Driver rubbed his hands on his thighs, looking uncomfortable. "How did it go?"

Cortland crossed his arms over his chest and uncrossed them as quickly. He didn't like talking about his issues, but it was Driver. "I don't know. Mostly, I just missed you."

"Then I ruined what could've been an amazing homecoming," Driver said, sounding sad.

Cortland shrugged. His gaze never wavered from Driver's sexy blue stare. "That remains to be seen, I guess."

"Are you saying the day can still be salvaged?"

The air seemed to get thinner, making it harder to breathe. "That depends."

"On?"

"If you stay over there," Cortland answered, refusing to backdown. He was finding that was the thing about human touch. It was addictive. Driver slipped from the bed and crossed the room. He stopped a foot away. "And now?"

"You're still too far away." The words came out in little more than a whisper. Driver's heated expression made it hard for Cortland to push words past his swollen throat. Damn, no one looked at him the way Driver did.

The final space between them disappeared as Driver's body collided with his. "Tell me how I can make us okay. You mean everything to me. The one thing I can't handle is losing you."

Cortland believed. Driver meant every word. It was in his eyes. Cortland needed his possessiveness. "Is it okay if I kiss you?"

At his question, Driver snagged the back of Cortland's neck and hauled him forward. Driver's mouth covered his. The towel wrapped around Cortland's hips wasn't anywhere near enough to hide his body's immediate reaction. Cortland tugged at Driver's shirt as the towel ripped away. Driver let Cortland have his shirt after tossing the towel over his shoulder. Cortland's feet left the floor as Driver cupped his ass and lifted him onto the dresser. Driver kissed and bit his way down Cortland's neck and chest. Cortland tilted his head back, giving Driver better access. Loud pants filled the air. Cortland held Driver's head between his hands, savoring every sensation.

A hint of reality sneaked its way in. "I don't have a single condom or anything."

Driver didn't slow. He stroked Cortland's erection as he nipped at Cortland's throat. "I'm totally clean, but there are half a dozen ways I can make love to you without needing protection. Trust me to take care of you."

Cortland's fingers dug into Driver's shoulders. "I trust you with everything."

At his claim, Driver's mouth covered his once more. Driver swept Cortland into his arms and headed for the bed. After settling Cortland on the mattress, Driver held Cortland's stare as he stripped. No one would ever know how much he'd missed the intense way Driver watched him. Driver's possessiveness made Cortland feel safe—like he'd never let anyone close enough to hurt Cortland.

Driver leaned over and kissed Cortland's stomach before climbing into bed. He crawled until he straddled Cortland's hips. Their erections bumped as Driver's mouth touched his. Their lips clung. Driver made no attempt to deepen their kiss. His lips brushed the corner of Cortland's mouth. Cortland automatically turned his head, chasing Driver's kiss. A soft chuckle vibrated against his skin as if he pleased Driver with the move. Cortland's palms landed on Driver's upper thighs. He massaged, savoring Driver's presence. Every day had been hell without him. Missing Driver had proven more to Cortland than counseling. He'd never turn away from Driver's touch. The craving was too big. Needing Driver eclipsed every other emotion inside him, taking over, and killing all the phobias standing in his way. At the end of the day, nothing or no one mattered to him more.

Driver moved against him. He reached between them and gently held their cocks in place as he rolled his hips. The sensation of their erections moving against each other had Cortland gasping for air. Driver kissed his neck, adding to the overload of pleasure.

"I love you." The whispered confession escaped Cortland without thought. The words needed to be free.

He felt Driver smile against his skin. "That's good. I don't want to be in love alone."

Cortland tugged at Driver's hair, forcing the man to meet his stare. "I'm sorry for going away for so long."

Driver went still. His intensity kicked up a notch. "Never apologize to me for taking care of yourself. I need to know you're good. You're the only thing keeping me sane."

The smile tugging at Cortland's lips was out of his control. "I'd like to drive you a little crazy."

Driver snorted. "You do that too."

While holding Cortland's gaze, Driver rolled his hips again. Cortland fought to keep his eyes open as the pleasure overtook him. He loved the way Driver's body felt against his. Driver's dick belonged where it was, stroking Cortland's. Cortland's hips lifted, seeking more. Needing more of Driver's brand of making love. Driver let him have it. His grip tightened on their erections. He stroked even as he rocked against Cortland, doubling the sensation of having his dick humped. Their mouths clashed as they strained to get closer. To feel more. Driver's teeth sank into Cortland's bottom lip as he ground down on Cortland, dragging a gasp from Cortland as pressure climbed up his shaft. His muscles tightened. He held his breath in anticipation. Driver tensed beneath Cortland's hands. Ragged breaths and moans filled the air. Driver threw his head back. His neck muscles visibly strained. Cortland couldn't look away. Hot cum coated Cortland's crown. An orgasm slammed into Cortland stealing all the oxygen from the room. Driver kept pumping, squeezing out every last spasm from Cortland. He dropped his forehead to Cortland's chest. His shoulders heaved as he visibly fought for air. Cortland couldn't stop touching Driver everywhere he could reach.

Driver licked Cortland's collarbone. "I should've held onto that towel."

Cortland shook with laughter. "Probably. I kind of like the idea of your cum mixing with mine. That was probably a weird thing to say," Cortland added, feeling stupid.

Driver lifted his gaze to Cortland's. His possessive edge hadn't lessened at all in the aftermath of his orgasm. "No." He dropped his weight, squishing the mess between their bodies. "This is probably the adult version of becoming blood brothers."

A loud laugh escaped Cortland without warning. He covered his nose and mouth, trying to smother the sound. Driver pushed his hand away and held it there, preventing Cortland from hiding. Cortland's smile wouldn't abate. Driver stared at him, looking hungry.

"Goddamn, you're breathtaking."

Driver's growled claim turned Cortland shy. His gaze skirted away. "You don't have to say that."

"It's true." Driver's intensity had Cortland's eyes sliding back his way. Driver didn't stop. "That day, when we met, I think about it all the time. You smelled good enough to eat, and you looked at me like no one else ever had. I didn't want you to leave. My life had been such a mess for so long, I'd forgotten what it felt like to have someone look at me like a man. I'd never seen eyes like yours. You probably won't believe it, but I think I loved you almost immediately. Definitely from the first time I saw you smile. There's no one else out there I want to be with." Driver shrugged. "You're the one for me."

Cortland's eyes stung. He nodded. "Same. If you're not terrified, you should be. I'm pretty convinced you belong to me now. I can sink pretty low when I'm trying to hang onto something that's mine."

Driver's bright smile made the confession worthwhile. "Same."

As Cortland looked on, Driver lowered his head.

He held Cortland's stare until the very last second before claiming his lips. The moment felt like a promise. Cortland held onto hope with both hands. God knew, he'd been starved of everything else for years.

SEVEN

"Where's Driver today?"

Everyone shrugged, looking unconcerned. With a sigh, Cortland went in search of his man. The building Micah rented as office space had about ten cubicles and a waiting room. Each person had a different job, from interviewing homeless candidates for the program to helping them find jobs and other services. Micah had really pulled off something amazing. Cortland was proud that Wyld had found such a great husband. Cortland liked knowing he could take part and help. It was always beyond fantastic that he could stop what he was doing and be with Driver at the drop of a hat. If he could find him that is.

Two months of officially dating had done

something Cortland hadn't thought possible. It had brought them closer. They'd already been best friends and spent every waking hour together. Now, instead of fantasizing about all the ways Cortland could have Driver, Driver let Cortland try whatever he wanted. He also hadn't thought it was possible to smile so much. Cortland definitely had never expected to be so happy. Now, twenty minutes after arriving at the home office of Micah's tiny home project, Cortland still hadn't spotted Driver. His texts were going unanswered and everyone he asked looked right through him. That was something Cortland was accustomed to dealing with. He knew he could lose his shit, showing the haughty temper Wyld had taught him to throw around, but Driver had to work with these people. Not to mention, most were volunteers. They couldn't lose those.

"He was here earlier, but I think he went home."

Cortland turned and focused on the blond guy who answered behind him. "Is everything okay?"

The guy shrugged. "He got a call and headed out. Driver doesn't really talk to anyone. It's hard to tell."

That didn't surprise Cortland. Driver was the quiet type. "Thank you. I'll check on him there."

"No problem. If he comes back, I'll tell him you were looking for him."

Cortland dipped his chin, acknowledging the guy's words. "Thanks again." He headed for the door. Driver didn't live that far. It took Cortland less than ten minutes to get to his house. While he'd been doing his stint in treatment, Driver had bought a truck. It wasn't sitting in the driveway. Still, Cortland jogged up the front steps and knocked. No answer came. Cortland turned in a slow circle. Something felt off today—like something bad was about to happen. A flash of light in the corner of Cortland's vision caught Cortland's eye. The dark-haired too-gorgeous-for-his-own-good guy from across the street jumped from his car and slipped inside his house. Cortland quickly crossed the road. He sifted through his memories, finally coming up with the man's name before knocking on the door. He knew Jonah was a friend of Driver's. It took everything he possessed to keep the jealousy to a minimum. It wasn't Jonah's fault he was younger and better than Cortland in every way.

As the door swung open, Jonah looked every bit as surprised to see Cortland as he should. He also looked like he'd been crying. His eyes and nose were red. Too bad that detail only made the guy hotter.

Cortland swallowed down an irritated sigh and dredged up a smile.

"Hi. Have you seen Driver today?"

"Sorry, no. I've been at school most of the day."

Cortland fought the urge to ask if he went to high school or college. Pettiness looked ugly on everyone. Almost as ugly as Cortland when he cried. His smile brightened to match his guilt. "Thanks. Sorry to bother you."

"You're not. I keep meaning to make the trip over to officially meet you, but I've been drowning in school work. Oh, hey, do you mind giving these sketches to Driver? I just haven't had time to visit."

"Um, sure," Cortland said, trying to keep up.

Jonah's expression filled with relief. "Thanks. You can come in while I grab them if you'd like?"

"Okay. Sure," Cortland said, slipping inside. He was immediately met by the tiny dog Jonah had been walking the night Cortland had propositioned Driver. Cortland had been so nervous that night, he'd forgotten that detail. He stared down at the dog. "Hi."

Jonah flashed him a smile as he stacked some frames together. "His name is Cricket. Don't worry. He doesn't bite."

Cricket was a hair bigger than Micah's dog, Bear,

but not much. The brown, fluffy guy sat on Cortland's shoe and refused to budge. "He's cute."

"Thanks," Jonah said, carrying the stack of frames his way. "I hate to give all this over to you, but I'm swamped."

"It's fine..." Cortland's attention locked on the images. They were his sketches. The ones he'd drawn for Driver. "These are mine."

Jonah nodded. "Like I said, I've had them since the day after John gave them back. It's my fault they weren't returned sooner. Speaking of which," Jonah said, sounding excited. "How do you feel about going to dinner with us one night? With Driver too, of course. You know John is a huge fan and he would die if you agreed to meet him."

Cortland blinked. "I don't know what's happening. Why did this John guy have to give Driver back my sketches?"

"Well, he didn't have to, but I talked him into it. Driver was such a fucking mess over having sold them to..." Jonah's expression changed, as if realization hit. "You didn't know he'd sold them, did you?"

Cortland shook his head.

Jonah covered his face. "Jesus fucking Christ." He dropped his hands and tilted his chin up to stare at the ceiling. "I'm such an idiot. It's like I'm failing at everything I touch."

"It's fine." In the face of Jonah's reaction, Cortland floundered. "Don't worry over it at all. I don't care if Driver sells them. They were a gift. If he found a buyer who actually wants them, it's fine."

Jonah blew out a breath. His obvious despair didn't lighten. "It's just that John wanted them, and John never takes no for an answer. Then, Driver was determined to move and sold them to finance his getaway but then he immediately regretted it, you know? I got them back, but now I'm just a goddamn idiot because he was so worried about upsetting you and then I fucking did it."

Cortland set the sketches aside and closed the distance between them. Without thought, he set his hands on Jonah's shoulders. "Stop. It's fine. Take a breath." Cortland's brain stuttered to a stop and froze. He was touching Jonah. It didn't hurt. He'd think that one over later. Right now, Jonah looked more than upset. He looked like he was choking on air. "I'm not bothered at all about the sketches. Stop worrying about that and tell me what's wrong."

Jonah focused on Cortland and sucked in a deep breath. It sounded ragged. "Sorry. I didn't mean to flip out like that. It's just that this is my senior year, and it's not looking like I'll graduate at the rate I'm going. Not that it matters because I don't have any desire to actually do anything my degree would let me do." The longer Jonah spoke, the more panicked he sounded again. "Most people have a plan, right? I don't have a fucking plan. John won't want me forever and I'm just fucking failing and useless at everything."

"Breathe," Cortland reminded him.

Jonah sucked in another breath. "Sorry," he said again. "Would you like something to drink?"

Cortland shook his head at Jonah's sad attempt to pretend he was fine. "Sit down. Does Cricket need to go out?" Cortland was in his element. He'd taken care of Wyld through drugged out stupors, benders, and just general overactive tangents millions of times.

Jonah shook his head. "He has a little doggie door in the back door. His bladder is too tiny to be home all day with no way to go out."

Cortland nodded and steered Jonah toward the couch. "That's one less thing. Now, sit. Everything can wait for a minute while you breathe. Point me in the right direction and I'll grab you a drink. Would you like tea or just something cold from the fridge?"

"You don't have to do that. Panic attacks have

become a common occurrence around here lately." Jonah sat, looking crestfallen. "Driver is lucky to have you. Usually, I'm alone for the worst of them."

A sad smile pulled at Cortland's lips. "I have a lot of personal experience with panic attacks, unfortunately."

Jonah's eyebrows rose. "I doubt that's true. You look very put together but thank you for trying to save my pride."

Cortland sat, choosing a spot on the couch near Jonah. "I look put together because that's always my first step in every day to holding my shit together. Now, do you want to talk about it, or is it too much for one conversation?"

"It's not that I don't want to talk about." Jonah shrugged, looking like he didn't know where to start. "Every time I try to put shit into words, it doesn't sound like anything anyone would understand. I mean, John and Driver both have amazing moms."

Cortland tried not to let his smile turn brittle. Had Jonah met Driver's Mom? Driver never even talked about his mom to Cortland. Thankfully, Jonah kept talking, saving Cortland from blurting out as much.

"I don't feel like I have anyone to talk to, because they're surrounded by great people. Meanwhile, I just spent two hours at my mom's house, crying, because even though she let me in the door, she wouldn't look at me or speak to me. She's my mom," Jonah said, sounding devastated. "I still need her and want her to hug me and tell me everything will be okay, but she doesn't want me. Not anymore."

As Cortland looked on, tears freely rolled down Jonah's cheeks. Something inside Cortland cracked. He understood. Maybe Driver and whoever this John guy was couldn't, but Cortland felt Jonah's words all the way to his soul. He moved closer and tugged Jonah in for a hug. He leaned back and let Jonah cry against his chest. Cortland knew he risked feeling like fire lashed at his skin by letting Jonah touch him, but he didn't care. Sometimes, there were more important things than physical discomfort.

"I won't say it's okay, because I know it's not."

He felt more than heard Jonah take a ragged breath. "She deserves for me to hate her and be enraged, but it's not in me. I'm just disappointed."

Cortland stared at a window to his right, seeing nothing but the ugly memories in his head. "I get it. When my dad died three years ago, I went to his funeral—like a dumbass. I thought it would give me closure or peace. Something. Of course, I knew my mom and brother would be there. All the way there,

I told myself it didn't matter. It wasn't about them. Then, I saw Mom and Brad holding each other beside my dad's open casket. It punched me in the chest. I couldn't breathe. It should've filled me with hatred to see them. Instead, I felt exactly like you described. They were my family. I wanted to be a part of them, but they didn't want me. No one wanted me. So, I left, feeling more alone than when I came."

"I want you."

Jonah and Cortland both jumped at the sound of Driver's voice. Jonah pulled away and swiped at his face while staring in the opposite direction. It couldn't have been more obvious he didn't want Driver to see him cry.

Cortland met Driver's stare. Even with the screen door standing between them, Cortland didn't miss that his features were every bit as hard as always, but there was something in his eyes. He looked like he was silently begging Cortland for everything.

"Hey, babe. I've been looking for you."

Driver stepped inside and pulled the screen door closed behind him. "One of our tiny home recipients had a job interview but no way to get there. I drove her there and back. When I got back to the office, I found my phone in my desk and saw you'd called. Mason said you'd come by and was headed here. Your car was empty in the driveway. I came to see if Jonah had seen you." His gaze slid Jonah's way and back again. "Is everything okay?"

Cortland answered, hoping to spare Jonah. "Yeah. Jonah had a rough day at school. We were talking it out."

"I'm fine now," Jonah said, coming to his feet and flashing a blatantly false smile. "Thank you for everything. I guess I'd better get in the shower. John is expecting me. Don't forget your sketches."

If Cortland hadn't been looking at Driver, he would've missed his reaction to Jonah's reminder. His features froze. He didn't appear to be breathing. His gaze moved between them, obviously unsure how to react.

"Thank you. I'll be sure to grab them on our way out," Cortland promised, ignoring the fact that Driver was visibly dying on the inside. "Let me leave my number with you. That way you can call anytime you need to talk."

Jonah nodded. He still looked a wreck. Cortland hated to leave him alone, but he obviously didn't like anyone to see him in this state. Cortland couldn't walk away without giving the boy a lifeline. He knew how having shitty parents could destroy a person. Cortland thought they could be friends. He kind of liked the idea of having someone else in the world.

ONCE JONAH PROGRAMMED Cortland's number in his phone, Driver helped Cortland gather the sketches. With a final wave to Jonah and pat for Cricket, they headed across the street. Driver didn't know where to start. They spent most of their time together at Cortland's, since it was Cort's job to be at Wyld's beck and call. Cortland hadn't mentioned the sketches he'd sent, and Driver hadn't found the time to retrieve them. He should've come clean. Now, he was dying inside for fucking up yet another thing and Cort acted like nothing happened. Driver had so much to say. First, he needed to explain why Jonah had the sketches and throw himself on Cortland's mercy.

"So, you sold my sketches to some guy named John," Cortland said before Driver could think of where to start.

Driver didn't know how he could possibly apologize for something so horrible. "I—"

"Honestly, I can't imagine you getting much for

them," Cortland said, cutting him off. "But they're yours and you're free to do what you want with them."

"I want them back on my walls." Driver gave Cortland a sharp nod as he made the claim. Money didn't matter anywhere near as much as Cortland's gift. A hint of discomfort trickled in. Now was the time to be completely honest. "I did sell him two of them, though. He was pretty desperate to have them. It seems you have a big fan. That's how I paid for my truck. Otherwise, I couldn't afford another monthly payment."

"Stop." So much humor filled that one word, Driver glanced Cortland's way. He was smiling. Driver couldn't look away. "Seeing this huge stack of framed sketches, what the hell was I thinking in the first place? You can't possibly have a place for all of these. I was just..." Cortland shrugged. "I missed you and I didn't have anything else to give you that you'd accept." Cortland's smile fell away. He looked sad in a way Driver hadn't seen in months. Driver needed to make the unhappiness go away, but Cortland kept talking, and showing more of his heart than usual. Driver needed that too. "If you'd let me, I'd give you the world." Cortland shook his head and leaned the sketches against the wall next to Driver's front door.

He straightened and met Driver's stare. His gorgeous amber-colored eyes were everything. Driver never got enough. "I guess that sounds trite. Not to mention, you really don't need me at all." Cortland blew out a loud breath as if things were quickly heading south. "Never mind. You probably have to get back to work and I just wanted to see you between errands for Wyld. I didn't mean to... forget it." Cortland turned away as if intent on leaving without even saying goodbye.

Panic slammed into Driver. Things had turned weird in the blink of an eye. "What the fuck? Hold up, Cort." Cortland stopped. His expression stabbed Driver through the heart. He looked wrecked and Driver had no fucking clue what had just happened. Driver rubbed Cortland's arms, needing to make things better. "Talk to me, baby. What's going on in your head?"

Cortland visibly swallowed. When he answered, his voice came out soft, as if it hurt to speak. "You don't need me for anything."

"Where's this coming from? My heart needs you. I thought you knew that."

Cortland's eyes fell closed. When they reopened, he looked defeated. "I guess it just kind of hit me. Jonah mentioned your mom, and you've never talked to me about your family. Then, I started talking about my mom, which brought up so much ugliness. I mean, I'm pretty damn unnecessary to everyone. What do I have to offer, really? Jonah says you have an amazing mom. I have no one. You obviously feel like you can talk to him about things you can't talk to me about, which sounds like I'm being petty when I say it aloud, but I'm not. It's just one more place I'm lacking. You don't want anything to do with my money. My art is just something to take up space. I'm just something that takes up space."

"Text Micah and tell him you have something you need to take care of. You're taking the rest of the day off." Even Driver heard the hard edge to his voice, but he couldn't control it.

Cortland shook his head. A sad smile touched his lips. "Just forget I said anything. It's not important."

"I'm not asking," Driver growled. He headed for the door, sweeping Cortland along with him. "You see, I've never really talked to you about my mom, because I care what you think of me. I don't care what Jonah thinks." He unlocked the door and muscled Cortland inside. "I get that I come off looking bad, because I chose to turn my back on my family when I came home a mess. More times than I can count, I've made my mom cry. I've forced her to beg me to come live with her and I still said no. She's pled with me to get help." Driver's throat burned with every confession, but he'd rather be the bad guy than let Cortland believe he didn't matter. Their relationship meant too much to him to stay silent. He locked the door behind him and toed off his shoes. Driver didn't look Cortland's way as the admissions flowed. "I've broken her heart more times than I can count. Honestly, I don't know why she still speaks to me. She keeps asking to meet you, but I keep making excuses, because I haven't wanted you to know I'm a terrible person." Driver pulled the tails of his shirt from his pants and unbuttoned it. He shrugged off the material. "I can't explain why I fought to get better for you when I wouldn't for her." Driver closed the distance between them and worked on the buttons of Cortland's shirt. Cortland stood still, letting it happen as Driver poured out his heart. "It scares the hell out of me that you might think less of me." When Cortland's shirt was completely unbuttoned, Driver tightened his hold on the two halves and hauled Cortland closer until they were nose to nose. His voice hardened. "Don't you ever try to tell me that I don't need you again. You are the only fucking thing holding my badly glued pieces together. Without you, I'd still be living in a tent. I'd still spend my whole day, trying to work up the nerve to end my life. Without you, I'm nothing."

"I should text Micah."

"Later," Driver growled, claiming Cortland's lips. All the rage he kept buried rose to the surface and manifested in their kiss. He nipped at Cortland's lips and sucked hard on his tongue. His hands found the man's ass and squeezed. He hauled Cortland against him, ensuring Cortland couldn't miss how hard he was for him. Driver was frustrated and hurting. Cortland's claims of being unwanted and unneeded rang loudly in his head. Driver was always hairbreadth away from insanity. Cortland was all that kept him tied to this world.

His pants loosened beneath Cortland's nimble fingers. Cortland didn't hesitate diving inside Driver's underwear and palming his cock. Driver tore at Cortland's clothes. It wasn't unusual for Driver to scare himself. He recognized his intensity was borderline insanity with Cortland. The man made him feel too much. Driver's possessiveness when it came to Cortland was terrifying. Cortland was his. He would be fucking happy with Driver. Cortland wasn't allowed to walk away. He sure as hell wasn't allowed to feel insecure in their relationship. This was everything.

"Do you feel it?" Driver asked, tearing at Cortland's clothes. "The desperation."

"Yes." The breathless note to Cortland's voice had carnal greed filling Driver to a boiling point.

"This is how I feel about you twenty-four-seven," Driver said. He held Cortland's face between his hands, forcing Cortland to hold his stare. "You're a madness beneath my skin. I love you more than I love anyone or anything. Even though I have nothing to offer other than myself, I still need you to understand this is forever. Maybe I don't have the details worked out, but you're mine."

Cortland looked turned on with his flushed cheeks and swollen lips. His eyes were slightly unfocused, but he didn't look scared. "I know," he said, blowing Driver away with his courage. "You should definitely take me to bed now."

"You should definitely sit on my face."

"Why aren't you leading the way?" Cortland shot back, pulling a chuckle from Driver.

"Let's go then." Driver took Cortland's hand and led him to the bedroom. Once there, they stripped in silence. Each time their gazes met, Driver's hunger grew. The instant he was nude, Driver fell backward onto the bed and motioned with his finger for Cortland to join him. As Cortland crawled onto the bed, Driver moved higher. "All the way up here, sexy. Use the headboard to brace yourself."

Cortland made him proud every time he didn't back down from a challenge. With one hand holding the headboard, Cortland didn't hesitate to straddle Driver's face. Driver's stomach growled. He was starving for Cortland. His cock leaked on his stomach. Driver ignored it. He didn't need anything like he craved tasting Cortland's dick.

Driver kissed Cortland's inner thigh. That's as far as his patience went. His hands found the globes of Cortland's ass. He spread the man's cheeks and dove in, licking and probing before giving Cortland's balls the same attention. Driver ignored Cortland's cock until the man practically begged. Cortland's crown was soaked with pre-cum. Cries and whimpers bounced from the walls. Finally, he licked Cortland from root to crown. Salty juices scraped across his tongue as he took Cortland to the back of his throat. Cortland's head was thrown back as he openly fucked Driver's willing mouth. He rocked, beating at Driver's throat. Cortland's muscles tensed. His movements turned frantic. Driver felt Cortland twitch, and he fisted Cortland's cock, choking off his orgasm before it hit.

A pained cry filled the air. Driver exploded into

action, flipping Cortland onto his back. He quickly lubed the man's ass and slammed inside. His hips slapped Cortland's ass as he pumped Cortland's cock, keeping the same rhythm. This time, when he felt Cortland tense, Driver didn't stop. Cortland's ass clamped down on his dick, nearly crippling him. Cortland's orgasm hit. His greedy ass sucked Driver deep with every spasm. Driver kept stroking, determined to massage every drop from Cortland. The pressure threatening his sanity exploded, stealing a loud cry from Driver. He pushed as deep as he could get inside Cortland—like imprinting on the man's soul. They were one in that moment. Driver fell forward and claimed Cortland's mouth. He couldn't get enough of this man. Driver wasn't sure if there was something stronger than love. If so, that's what they were. They were incomplete with each other—both on the verge of insanity. Together, they were different. Stronger. There was nothing they couldn't conquer.

DRIVER KEPT KISSING the back of Cortland's neck, making him crazy. Goosebumps covered his skin. Cortland was beginning to think they'd be permanent. Not to mention, it was making it hard as hell to make a sandwich for the man. Cortland had been rendered completely useless by Driver's lips minutes earlier. Now, all he could do was cling to the counter and feel. With his chin down, eyes closed, and panting for breath, Cortland reveled in the sensation of Driver's lips caressing his nape.

A loud knock sounded, dragging a groan from Cortland. "No." Even to his ears, it sounded like a plea.

Driver didn't stop. Cortland chuckled. It was obvious Driver had no intention of answering the door. The knock sounded again.

"They're not going away."

Driver growled against Cortland's skin, making it even harder to breathe. "I'll get rid of them."

Cortland nodded. He hoped Driver got rid of them quick. Cortland didn't move. He wanted Driver's lips back.

"Driver."

Cortland jumped at the booming voice, coming from the living room. Sam popped up from where he warmed Cortland's feet to scramble for the living room. Curiosity piqued, Cortland followed at a slower pace. A mountain of a man stood in the doorway. Even though he was solid muscle, he was easily the friendliest looking person Cortland had ever seen. He had deep laugh lines around his eyes and was smiling bright. Cortland spotted Jonah squashed to the man's side.

"Oh my god. Hey," the mountain said as he caught sight of Cortland.

Cortland blinked in surprise. "Hey."

"Hey, Cortland. This is John," Jonah said, speaking up.

"Oh, hey." All the talk of John made sense now. Apparently, they were a couple. Oddly, they fit. Jonah looked tiny next to John, but they looked happy together. That mattered. "It's nice to meet you."

Driver moved aside and waved the couple inside. "Come in."

John's excitement was tangible. For some reason Cortland couldn't explain, he couldn't stop smiling. It was like John brought the sunshine. He half expected the man to barrel him over. Instead, John stopped short of colliding with him. He kept one arm wrapped around Jonah and the other behind his back. "Sorry to burst in on you. Jonah told me at dinner he'd met you today and your car was still here when we got home. I'm a huge fan of your work."

That explained why John made a show of not

shaking hands. Thanks to that damn candid interview Wyld had convinced him to do, he had no secrets. Cortland felt suddenly shy. He wanted to look away. A blush climbed up his cheeks. Art was a private thing to him. He didn't usually meet fans. In truth, even though his work sold, he didn't think he had fans, per se. "Oh. Um, thank you."

"I don't want to be over the top, but—"

"He's being modest. John's always over the top," Jonah said, cutting in.

John nodded. "He's not lying. So, I'll just be me. Do you have a private collection for sale, or one I could see sometime?"

Cortland was taken slightly aback. He had lots of sketches people had never seen. They were nothing special. "I suppose. If you're interested, I'm sure I can figure something out."

Somehow, John's smile kicked up a notch. "Can I leave my number with you, or get yours, so we can set something up?"

"Jonah has my number. I'm fine with whatever."

"Woot," John yelled, lifting Jonah off his feet in his enthusiasm and pulling a laugh from the guy.

Cortland's cheeks ached. John was exactly what Jonah needed after the way his shitty mother had treated him. He hoped one day John stole Jonah away from everything. The way Jonah looked at John with his heart in his eyes said he wouldn't mind if he did.

Driver moved behind Cortland and wrapped his arms around him, pulling Cortland back against his chest.

Jonah's gaze swung Cortland's way. "We'll let you two get back to your night. Thank you for taking a minute to meet John. You've made his night."

John nodded. "You have."

Cortland nodded at them both. "It was great seeing you. Just let me know when you want to get together."

With a final round of goodbyes, Jonah dragged John from the house. Driver kept a tight hold on Cortland. His lips found Cortland's nape again. Cortland felt him smile against his skin. "My famous, sexy baby. I can't wait to get such a popular man in bed."

"In that case," Cortland said, taking his hand and heading for the bedroom. "We can eat later."

"Yes!" Driver's excited hiss had Cortland's smile turning into a chuckle. Cortland had never imagined this life for himself. Now, he couldn't picture his life any other way.

EIGHT

With Cortland's back turned, Driver quickly scribbled on the dry erase board Wyld kept on the refrigerator door. Since they'd be leaving for the store soon, Driver knew Cortland would check the board before they left. He jumped away from it before Cortland caught him. When Cortland turned, Driver grabbed a mug and headed for the coffeemaker. It took all his self-control not to watch Cortland's every move.

"Hmmm, I wonder why Wyld wants me to pick up more time with Driver from the store?"

Driver glanced over to find Cortland's eyes swimming with mirth. Still, he played the innocent by shrugging. "I don't know. Maybe he thinks you should keep me around."

Cortland crossed the room and crowded Driver's space. "What do you think? Do you think I should keep you around?"

Driver loved the playful glint in Cortland's eyes. In the seven months since they'd shared that kiss at Micah's fundraiser, he'd watched Cortland blossom. He smiled more than he didn't. Cortland's happiness healed Driver a little more every day. It proved Driver didn't destroy everything he touched. "You should definitely keep me around. Otherwise, I'll fall into doldrums, stop eating, bathing, or functioning as an adult in any way. When I'm scrawny and stinky, people will throw rocks at me in the street, and it'll be all your fault."

The sexy rumble of laughter coming from Cortland had Driver towing him closer. He wanted to feel the sound's vibration against his chest. "You're the most dramatic person I know."

"I doubt that," Driver argued as he kissed Cortland's neck. His fingers automatically curled around Cortland's belt. He was already trying to decide how to convince Cortland to go back to bed with him and they hadn't been up that long. Cortland lured Driver in for a kiss. As always, it turned hotter faster than anticipated. He urged Cortland backward, trying to maneuver him inside the pantry so he could take advantage of him. The jingle of Sam's collar had a groan rising in his throat. That sound could only mean Micah was coming. Since they practically lived there now, Sam stayed glued to Micah's side. It was obvious the dog sensed what Driver had always known—Micah was really an angel living among men.

He heard Micah fussing before he cleared the doorway. "If I put him down, you have to be careful," Micah said, sounding exactly like he was talking to a child. "Bear is still a baby, and you're a big guy. Don't crush him."

As Driver looked on, Sam clapped his front paws, begging for Micah to put down the tiny dog.

After giving Sam a stern nod, Micah set Bear on the kitchen floor. The minuscule dog immediately attacked Sam's ears. The way Sam stayed on his side with his tongue hanging out proved he wasn't bothered. Obviously appeased, Micah focused on them.

"Good morning, guys. How is everyone today? You both look happy."

Driver imagined that was true. He could feel the smile stretching his lips, but he couldn't force it away. Instead, he hauled Cortland against his side, refusing to the let man have any peace. Before either of them could respond, Wyld strolled into the kitchen completely nude.

Driver averted his gaze.

Micah snagged a nearby apron they kept for just these occasions. He quickly wrapped the material around Wyld's hips and tied it. "Sorry," he mouthed over Wyld's shoulder, pulling a chuckle from Driver.

"Angel, this is my house. What's the point in having truckloads of money if I can't walk around my own house naked?"

"You have guests." He kissed Wyld's shoulder. "Otherwise, I wouldn't mind."

"They're not guests," Wyld argued, grumbling like a child, but he let Micah have his way.

Driver got it though. "Actually, he has a point," Driver said, throwing out his two cents. "This is an amazing house. I can't imagine what it cost, but it should definitely give him the right to walk around nude."

Wyld nodded. "Exactly so. I knew I liked you for a reason."

"The rest of us just have to adopt a locker room, rain locker mentality," Driver added.

"See?" Wyld said, sounding triumphant. "Driver gets it."

"Slightly off topic," Micah said, obviously ready to

drop the matter of Wyld's nudity. "I think you should move in, Driver. Obviously, we have the room. You can save your money and Cortland's here. There's really no reason for you to keep a separate house."

Wyld blinked. He looked confused for a moment. "You already live here, don't you? I'm fairly certain you do."

"No, but I plan to ask Cortland to marry me, so it's a tho—"

"Then you definitely live here," Wyld said, refusing to let him finish. "No other assistant will put up with me. I'll hire you too, if that's what it takes to keep Cortland from leaving."

"Technically, Driver already works for you," Micah reminded Wyld with a chuckle.

"Whoa," Cortland said, cutting in. "Why is this the first I've heard of you planning to ask me to marry you? Shouldn't I have been the first to know of this plan?"

Driver was having fun. He liked it here. It was like happiness lived in this house. "I've told you several times we are forever, haven't I?"

Cortland's incredulous expression never wavered. "Yeah, but that's not the same as an actual marriage proposal."

"That's because I haven't done it yet."

Cortland blinked several times, making Driver wonder if he planned to stab him. "Fine. Maybe I'll say yes when you do."

A chuckle rose in Driver's throat. "I guess we'll find out sooner or later."

Cortland nodded and added some creamer to his coffee. Driver took a drink to hide his smile. Of course, Cortland had perfected it with the creamer. Cortland always made everything better. Driver didn't last long.

"Hey, Cort."

Cortland lifted his gaze from the cup he was making for himself. His eyebrows rose in question. "What, baby?"

"Would you like to get married today?"

The way Cortland's lips twitched had Driver biting the inside of his cheek to keep from laughing. "I don't know. I'll have to check my boss' schedule. Boss?" Cortland said, focusing on Wyld.

Everyone focused on Wyld. He looked thoughtful. "I'll pay for your marriage license and a two-week honeymoon anywhere you want to go, if you'll both agree to live here, and Cortland has to agree to never leave me."

"Awww," Cortland cooed, sounding touched. "I love you too, Wyld."

Driver understood. Wyld wasn't sentimental with anyone other than Micah, but Cortland and Wyld cared about each other. They were family. Driver would never expect Cortland to leave the home where he'd found so much security. Not to mention, he doubted anyone would pay Cortland so much to do so little. In truth, Driver believed Wyld paid Cortland just to live there. Wyld rarely expected anything from Cortland, and Cortland had been running Wyld's household for so long it ran itself.

"It looks like I'm free," Cortland said, taking a sip of his coffee.

Driver had a hard time hanging onto his nonchalant air. He'd never expected to marry. Driver had doubly never expected Cortland to agree to marry him. "I love you." Driver's voice shook as he made the confession.

Cortland quickly set his cup aside and closed the distance between them. "I know, baby. Don't worry. You'll be a great husband. I'm not scared."

He loved the way Cortland always read his mind, going straight to the heart of his fears.

"Come on, sexy," Micah said, leading Wyld from

the kitchen. "Let's go jump on the bed and let these two have some privacy."

"Oooh, you had me at come," Wyld said, his voice floating down the hall.

The moment they were alone, Driver cupped Cortland's face. He searched the man's gaze, looking for any sign he wasn't ready for this. Cortland's eyes were clear. He was calm. "I don't want to rush you."

"You're not."

Driver couldn't let it go. "I also don't want you to feel like you're stuck with a crazy person."

"I don't."

Cortland sounded so sure. His confidence in them was the sexiest sight Driver had ever witnessed. It fed Driver's already firm belief they would be amazing. "No one could love you more," Driver whispered, because he needed Cortland to know.

"Same," Cortland whispered back before touching his lips to Driver's. It felt like they'd already exchanged vows. For Driver, every word exchanged between them meant the world. To anyone else, they might seem a little broken. In truth, they filled each other's cracks, making the other whole. No one could tear them apart or come between them. Together they were complete. They were one heart.

KEEP an eye out for the next Sugar Daddies, *Sugar Protector*.

PLEASE CONSIDER LEAVING a review at the retailer where this book was purchased. Reviews really help with a book's visibility, which ensures I can continue writing. Thank you, Charity.

ABOUT THE AUTHOR

Charity Parkerson is an award winning and multi-published author with several companies. Born with no filter from her brain to her mouth, she decided to take this odd quirk and insert it in her characters.

*Eight-time Readers' Favorite Award Winner
  *2015 Passionate Plume Award Finalist
  *2013 Reviewers' Choice Award Winner
  *2012 ARRA Finalist for Favorite Paranormal Romance
  *Five-time winner of The Mistress of the Darkpath

Connect with her online:

--Join my street team: facebook.com/TeamCharityParkerson
  --Sign up for my newsletter: http://bit.ly/CharityNews

--Website: charityparkerson.com

--Facebook:

facebook.com/authorCharityParkerson

facebook.com/TheMenofSin

--Twitter: twitter.com/CharityParkerso

www.ingramcontent.com/pod-product-compliance
Lightning Source LLC
Chambersburg PA
CBHW061251170626
46809CB00007B/2947